CW00798386

070 893 673 371 02

Love is
a time of enchantment:
in it all days are fair and all fields
green. Youth is blest by it,
old age made benign:
the eyes of love see
roses blooming in December,
and sunshine through rain. Verily
is the time of true-love
a time of enchantment — and
Oh! how eager is woman
to be bewitched!

SEVEN DAYS FROM MIDNIGHT

In the Comet Theatre, London, seven people have good reason for wanting beautiful Maxine Culver out of the way: Grace Challoner, leading lady, and her politician husband, Philip Dunster; Stephen Hammond, her leading man; Ethel Fothergill, the character actress; and old Tom Langley, stage director. Each one has reason to fear Maxine's blackmail, but perhaps none so much as Doctor David Radcliffe, whose first play is being produced at the Comet, and who has fallen in love with fledgling actress Susan Howard . . . But whose shadow is it that lurks in the wings, waiting to silence Maxine once and for all?

Books by Rona Randall
Published by The House of Ulverscroft:

RONA RANDALL

SEVEN DAYS FROM MIDNIGHT

Complete and Unabridged

ULVERSCROFT
Leicester

First published in Great Britain

First Large Print Edition
published 1997

British Library CIP Data

Randall, Rona
    Seven days from midnight.—Large print ed.—
Ulversrcroft large print series: romance
    1. English fiction—20th century
    2. Large type books
    I. Title
    823.9'14 [F]

    ISBN 0–7089–3673–3

Published by
F. A. Thorpe (Publishing) Ltd.
Anstey, Leicestershire
Set by Words & Graphics Ltd.
Anstey, Leicestershire
Printed and bound in Great Britain by
T. J. Press (Padstow) Ltd., Padstow, Cornwall

This book is printed on acid-free paper

1

"**M**IDNIGHT," said Maxine Culver as the strokes of Big Ben echoed across Westminster. Then she added with a dazzling smile, "Telephone Grace Challoner now. Tell her she's got to do this — or else. Understand?"

"Can blackmail ever be misunderstood?" Ethel Fothergill replied.

Maxine laughed. Like her smile it was bright and attractive, but like her smile it contained no warmth.

"Telephone her right away," she commanded.

"On a Sunday night? I'll do no such thing."

"I think you will, darling." Casually, Maxine dangled a newspaper cutting between thumb and forefinger. "In fact, I'm quite sure you will."

"But it's after midnight!"

"Midnight exactly. Can't you hear Big Ben?"

1

Ethel could. From her little flat above a shop on Millbank she could hear the deep booms echoing from their tower. The sound of Big Ben, the roar of Embankment traffic and the throb of river vessels were a muted accompaniment to her life, and to a permanency which she had never dreamed could be hers.

For the last six years, thanks to the steady employment given her by the Comet Theatre Company, she had lived in this modest place — warm, comfortable, conveniently situated, a real home. Otherwise her existence would have been the precarious one of an ageing actress — seasons in provincial rep., supporting rôles in TV plays when she could get them, and an occasional part in a West End production if she was lucky. But one day, after years in which their paths had ceased to cross, she had met Grace Challoner walking across Parliament Square, and after that, insecurity had gone whistling down the wind, for Grace saw her and hurried across calling: "Ethel! Dear Ethel, where *have* you been all these years?"

Haunting the agents' offices. Taking

what jobs she could get. Playing the heavies in provincial rep. All the things that a middle-aged character actress had to do to keep body and soul together, but never battening on to friends who had gone up in the world.

Once upon a time she and Grace had toured together, sharing dressing-rooms and lodgings; once upon a time she had been like a mother to the girl, but a lot of water had passed under the bridge since then, carrying Grace to leads in London and New York and finally marriage to a man very much in the public eye. As wife of a leading politician she was elevated far above Ethel in the social scale — or so thought Ethel.

But Grace's delight on meeting her again had been genuine.

"I'm not going to let you disappear into the blue this time," she declared. "Come to the Comet Theatre tomorrow morning. Philip and I have formed a resident company there, so it's good-bye to films and travelling for me from now on. Running the Comet is something I can do in conjunction with running a home. We hate separations, so Philip is providing the financial backing for the new venture and Stephen Hammond is to be my leading man."

And that started it. For six years the *avant garde* theatre, resurrected from the old-time Comet Music Hall, had maintained its cultural hold on London's theatrical world, with a flourishing stage partnership between Grace Challoner and Stephen Hammond, old Tom Langley as resident stage director, and Ethel Fothergill as resident character actress. Even when there was no part for her in a current production she remained on the payroll. Grace had been a staunch friend, but when thanked she brushed it aside.

"I owe you a lot, and I haven't forgotten. You were the only friend I had, once upon a time."

But Ethel had ceased to think of that time. It was in the past, known only to herself and Grace. Or so she had thought, until now.

"Telephone her," Maxine repeated, picking up the receiver and handing it across.

Ethel took the receiver and dropped it back.

"I need time," she fenced.

"There isn't time. Didn't you say that auditions start to-morrow?"

"I can't ring her at this hour."

"Why not?" Maxine's ripe mouth curved suggestively. "Are you worrying in case she and Philip Dunster are in bed? I doubt it. I walked past their house on my way here, to check up. Lights were still blazing."

"I wish you weren't my sister's child," Ethel said steadily, "because then I wouldn't feel any guilt about disliking you the way I do."

Maxine threw back her lovely head and laughed.

"Don't try to kid me, or yourself, that you're giving in because of our relationship, darling. You are thinking of your own precious skin. *And* all this." Her glance took in the attractive sitting-room, the shelves lined with books, the deep armchairs, the few choice pictures, the rare porcelain collected slowly and with pleasure over the years — the whole implication of permanency which the place gave out. And permanency to an ageing actress was something worth

5

fighting for. It was unbearable to think that with one malicious gesture this girl might sweep it all aside.

"Nevertheless," Ethel answered honestly, "I'm not thinking of myself, but of Grace as well. She is happily married."

"*And* successful. And quite stinkingly rich. Why should she have everything?"

"She has worked hard."

"So have hundreds of others. So have I. Anyway, I'm not out to rob her, she won't be deprived of a thing. All I want is a part in the new play. Why should she object?"

"You will have to take an audition, if I can get you one."

"I'll face any audition provided I get the part at the end of it. I'm not an amateur, you know."

"Then why couldn't your agent have fixed it for you?"

"Darling, I've quarrelled with my agent." Maxine's slim shoulders shrugged. "Come to that, there isn't an agent in London I haven't quarrelled with at some time or another."

"So none of them will handle you now. I see."

6

"That's no loss. Agents are useless, anyway. I prefer to go after parts for myself."

"Or blackmail others into getting them for you?"

"Call it what you like, my darling aunt, so long as you get me in."

Ethel answered uneasily, "I can't guarantee it. All I can ask for is an audition, and I expect the queue will be long."

"Then you'd better arrange for me to jump it." Maxine studied the newspaper cutting thoughtfully. "I wonder how Philip Dunster and his aristocratic family would survive the shock of this. It would create quite a scandal, and I'm willing to bet that Grace Challoner would do anything to avoid one."

Ethel said with disgust, "What a vicious creature you are! How often have you done this sort of thing — scavenging around amongst people's lives, hoarding facts like a human jackdaw until you could use them to your advantage?"

"Don't moralise." Maxine suppressed a yawn. "Just do as I tell you. Telephone now — or else." The threatening note

7

in her elocutionised voice deepened. "I wonder what would become of those on the payroll of the Comet Theatre Company if anything happened to break it up?"

"You can't be sure that it would break up."

"I could have a damned good try. Not that I want to — I am *not* vicious, contrary to what you think — but what a story this would make, just when a new production is coming along! I hear it's a good play. By an unknown doctor, isn't it?"

"So you know that, too."

"Darling, these things get around. I read it in some theatre column somewhere." Maxine picked up the telephone receiver and held it out again. "Time's passing," she warned. "Don't waste any more of it. You'll be sorry, if you do."

2

GRACE CHALLONER was preparing for bed. She had a busy day ahead of her, auditioning from ten o'clock onwards, and Philip had to attend a political conference at eleven, which meant that he had to call at the House of Commons to deal with mail beforehand. So they had both resolved to go to bed early to-night and, like many other nights, time had slipped by and here it was, midnight already.

Somehow they always took their time over going to bed on Sundays, chatting desultorily, making plans, talking as husbands and wives do talk when drifting off to bed after a leisurely week-end. It was the rhythm of a firmly established marriage, shutting out the world.

So the harsh summons of the telephone at this hour was startling and unwelcome.

She picked up the white receiver beside their bed and heard Ethel Fothergill's voice say, "Grace dear, I'm sorry to ring so late, but I wanted to ask a favour of you. I'm afraid it won't wait until morning."

As usual, it was pleasant to listen to Ethel. She had the warm, deep voice of a middle-aged character actress but, even more, the warmth of a friend.

Because of their long and close association Grace answered promptly. "That's all right, Ethel. You know I'll do anything for you."

She heard a suppressed sigh of relief from the other end of the line, and asked quickly, "What's the matter? Is something wrong?"

"No — no! What could be?"

"Then that's all right. What's the favour?"

"I want you to audition someone to-morrow."

"A girl, I take it? We're auditioning for the part of Nina."

"I know, and this girl is not inexperienced. Thank you for agreeing."

Grace laughed. "Well, it isn't much of a favour, lining a girl up with a hundred others to say some lines and take a chance."

"The favour," said Ethel carefully, "is in casting her."

"You mean irrespective of whether she can act or not? Overriding others who have slogged to get a chance in London? Oh come, Ethel, it can't be done, and you know it. It wouldn't be fair, not only to the other poor hopefuls, but to the play — not to mention the Comet. You know we never do things that way. Influence cuts no ice with us. A person must have talent, or they're out. And how can you ask such a thing for the part of Nina? Second lead!"

"Not even the second matters when you are playing first."

"I don't agree. What's come over you, Ethel? It isn't like you to ask such a favour."

"You agreed," Ethel insisted. "You said you would do it."

"I said I'd give her an audition, no more."

"You said you'd do anything. *Anything*, Grace."

"Be reasonable! Surely it is enough to give the girl a chance with the rest? If she's good enough, she will get the part.

If not . . . " Grace's lovely shoulders lifted in a shrug which Ethel could well imagine. A shrug of pity, and of dismissal. "You may as well warn her that she'll be up against pretty stiff opposition. Stephen saw a girl in a RADA performance he was judging, a girl named Susan Howard. She carried off the Bronze Medal and he asked her to come along to-morrow. He is dead set on having her for the part. He says she's another Dorothy Tutin."

"But you haven't signed her up yet?"

"Of course not. *I* have to see her perform first. Anyway, tell this girl of yours to come along to-morrow. We're starting at ten and the list is a mile long, so she'll have to be at the end of it."

There was a hint of desperation in Ethel's voice as she pleaded, "Grace, *please* cast her. If you would guarantee it you don't know how grateful I'd be."

Grace frowned, feeling puzzled, disturbed, and a little tired.

"Darling," she sighed, "how can I? I haven't even seen the girl act. By the way, who is she?"

After a split second's silence Ethel said, "My niece."

"Maxine Culver! Oh, no!"

"You promised."

"But you didn't mention her name! You merely asked me to do you a favour. Was that fair?"

"Why should you mind? Have you anything against her?"

"Not a thing personally, I only know her reputation. So do you, even though she is your niece. Maxine is a trouble maker, and every cast she has worked with has finished up by hating her."

Ethel said urgently, "If you give her the part I'm sure you won't regret it, but if you don't — you might."

"I think that very unlikely," Grace answered dryly. "Maxine is a competent actress, but so are many others who mercifully lack her talent for mischief-making. Frankly, I can't understand why you suddenly plead for her, because I've always felt that despite your relationship there's no love lost between you. And what has made her come back into your life? I thought you had completely lost touch."

13

That was true. Ethel hadn't seen or heard of her niece for several years, and her unexpected arrival had been an unpleasant surprise.

She answered vaguely, "She's been away on tour," but wasn't really sure whether this was so. Maxine had skilfully dodged personal questions. Ethel continued urgently, "She hasn't had a 'shop' in town for ages. I feel sorry for her. Please help her, Grace."

"Well, I sympathise with any actress who is down on her luck, but if we were to cast our plays with all the actors we feel sorry for, every Comet production would be a flop. Anyway, the decision doesn't rest entirely with me. Stephen has a certain say in these matters."

"But the authority is yours. It is your company."

Grace was troubled by the note of urgency in Ethel's voice. It suggested desperation, and suddenly the line was as taut as a violin string.

"The most I will do," Grace repeated, "is to arrange for her to be auditioned."

"Well, thank you for that, at least."

14

Ethel's voice departed on an uneasy note.

★ ★ ★

Philip Dunster came into the bedroom as his wife finished talking. He was a vigorous man several years older than she, of medium height, stockily built, with mouth and eyes revealing kindly humour. He wore a Paisley silk dressing-gown over pyjamas.

"Who was that?" he asked.

"Ethel Fothergill."

Grace's hand was still on the telephone and she was frowning a little.

"Rather late for a let-your-hair-down gossip, wasn't it?"

Philip dropped a kiss on the crown of her blonde head, and her heart warmed to him. She loved this man deeply.

Even after ten years she was still surprised at finding herself married into the brilliant Dunster family. Their name had been known in political circles for three generations, whereas her own people had never been famous and were never likely to be. She didn't count her own success as an actress, believing that luck and a measure of good looks had been responsible for that. Characteristically she underrated her ability, even though it would have placed her in the foreground of her profession without beauty as an additional asset.

Philip stood behind her, loosening the coil of her hair.

"The thing I love about you," he said, "is your capacity for remaining unchanged. You had long hair when I met you — how many years ago? Is it really more than ten? — and you have never cut it. Not that I would let you, of course." He smiled, his eyes crinkling at the corners. "And it's still the same lovely colour, like wheat with the sun upon it."

"Aided and abetted by my hairdresser!"

She spoke lightly, but Philip's hands dropped to her shoulders and remained there. "What has Ethel said to upset you?" he asked quietly.

Slowly, Grace began to wield a hairbrush.

"Nothing, really. She merely wants me to audition someone and I don't want to do it."

"Then don't."

"But she begged me to as a personal favour. She even tried to persuade me to guarantee the part."

"That's absurd," Philip protested. "Give the girl — is it a girl? — an audition and let it go at that. If Ethel is disappointed, she'll get over it. She'll have her own part in the play, so why should she really care?"

Philip's hands caressed the back of his wife's neck. "This is the bit I like," he said, crooking his finger in a strand of hair and letting it spring back gently. He kissed the spot where it fell, then said, "While you're doing your nightly hundred I'll have a cigarette."

He stretched out on the bed, watching her through a trail of smoke. Grace disliked smoking in the bedroom, but never had the heart to tell him so. Mutual tolerance was part of the bond between them; they had achieved the contentment of a well-adjusted marriage. Now the heavy brocade curtains were drawn against the night, enclosing them in their private world.

He rolled on to one side, the better

to watch her. This nightly brushing of her hair held a rhythmic fascination for him.

"It is almost ridiculous, the way I still love you," he murmured.

"There's nothing ridiculous about love," she answered, "I find it very satisfactory."

"That makes two of us."

He was lucky and he knew it. He had a home which really was a home, and a wife who really was a wife.

Politicians depended on their wives to an almost alarming extent. The right wife, they said, was important to a man's career. She must be politically minded, putting her husband's job before all things; self-effacing, hard working, always in the background of his life. In other words, the muted accompaniment to his solo performance.

So naturally, when he married an actress, his family predicted disaster. Their interests would clash, they warned him. She would put her career first, and in any case theatrical limelight had often been damaging to a man in politics. What he needed was a woman from a similar background to his own.

18

The trouble with the Dunster family, Philip had decided long ago, was the way in which they took it for granted that he would follow their pattern, both career-wise and marriage-wise, so naturally they had not taken kindly to his choice of a wife, and naturally they would not acknowledge, even now, that his choice had been good. He had a sneaking suspicion that they hated to admit that his marriage had been far more successful than any of theirs.

"Who is this girl Ethel wants you to audition?"

"Her name is Maxine Culver, a niece, and I think the girl is trading on the relationship."

"It sounds as if you don't like her."

"I don't."

"Do I know her?"

"I don't think you've ever met. You would remember her, if so. No one could forget Maxine."

"Has she worked for Comet?"

"No. At one time she was quite well known in the profession — never leads, but working up that way. She might have got somewhere if she hadn't caused trouble wherever she went. In every production it was the same — within a few weeks unrest spread through the cast. In the end, managements regarded her as a Jonah and gave her a wide berth. I thought she had vanished into oblivion, but suddenly she has turned up again. I don't want her in this play. It's a good one, and young Doctor Radcliffe is too nice to have his first play marred by a Jonah. He doesn't deserve it."

Grace put aside her hairbrush and crossed to the bed. Philip pulled her down beside him, feeling the softness of her body beneath a flimsy nightdress, and promptly they forgot about Maxine Culver.

But later, when Philip was asleep, Grace lay awake, thinking of Ethel, and Maxine, and of the theatre which, next to Philip, was her greatest love; of the new play, and Ethel's extraordinary request. The urgency in her voice echoed in Grace's memory. *As a personal favour to me, take on Maxine . . .* '

Vicious, predatory, scheming — that was Maxine Culver and everyone knew it, including her aunt, so there must be some deeper motive behind Ethel's insistence. Was Maxine persuading her, forcing her?

But that was blackmail and why should anyone blackmail a woman whose past couldn't be more respectable?

Unlike mine, thought Grace with a mental shiver.

3

"MIDNIGHT," said Susan Howard as Big Ben boomed across Westminster, echoing as far as the narrow side street in Victoria where she shared two top rooms with Della Kent, a fellow drama student.

"Then it's time you were in bed. You've to rise and shine early to-morrow, don't forget. What time is the audition?"

"The call is for ten o'clock, but how far down the list I am I've no idea. As for forgetting, I can think of nothing else!"

Susan moved restlessly, leaning on the window-sill and staring out across night-lit London. Normally the scene fascinated her, conjuring up comparisons with her home town in the North. By now the streets of Arkley would be dark, its inhabitants asleep, including her parents. Dad had to be up and away early on Mondays, clocking in at the factory at eight, and he walked the four miles from home because he had always done so. "Keeps me fit, keeps me young," he always said, and maybe he was right, although if walking did that for him the foot-slogging Mother did in that shop ought to be a rejuvenation course. Instead, she had fallen arches and thick ankles and an aching back. Even so, she never grumbled.

"The money's a godsend," she said, and so it was — all eight pounds of it. Eight pounds for forty hours — how much was that per hour? Susan tried to work it out, but couldn't. Maths had never been her subject — more's the pity, said Dad, who visualised his girl becoming something ambitious, like a school teacher.

"Now *there's* a career for you," he always said. "Good pay and security. What more d'you want? This acting lark is all very well for folks with money, but what're you going to live on when you're not acting?"

What, indeed? She had asked herself that question a thousand times. The profession was overcrowded, a rat-race with no room for scruples or morals, and she possessed both.

23

"If I fail at this audition to-morrow," she mused aloud, "I don't know what I'll do."

"You won't fail," declared Della.

The girls had lived together for two years and their friendship was a close one — surprisingly so, considering they were such opposites. Opposites in every way; looks, background, schooling, the lot. Why Della wanted to rough it in two top rooms in the poorer part of Victoria when she could live in luxury at home in Knightsbridge was something Susan had given up trying to understand, but there it was — Della had made the gesture and had stuck to it. That it was no more than a gesture Susan had been convinced when, two years ago, Della had asked her to double up.

"You'll like it better than the students' hostel," she had urged. "Try it and see."

"You'll tire of it and of me," Susan had urged, making a feeble attempt at resistance. The attempt failed. She hated the hostel; the rooms that were virtually dormitories, the lack of privacy, the supervision which made her feel

24

that she was back at school, not even adult. The thought of being free and independent, and the miracle of being offered a room at a price she could afford, had an overpowering appeal. A room of her own, attic though it was, bare though it was, was worth going without things for. Cigarettes, make-up, the money-wasters which other girls took for granted, these could go by the board, and the grant which her drama scholarship carried would just about take care of the rest.

And if Della did tire and went scuttling home to Lowndes Square and luxury, the room would be snapped up by someone else, so what had she to lose by the experiment?

She didn't lose, and Della didn't tire. Pampered, petted and spoilt as she was, she debunked both her parents' predictions and Susan's doubts. "How much've you got to live on?" she demanded. "Then that's what I will live on, too." And she did. And managed. And liked it.

"I don't know what you're worrying about," she said now. "A scholarship

25

student, plus a bronze medal! They ought to jump at you. And don't forget that the divine Stephen Hammond particularly asked for you."

"That doesn't mean that I'm in. There are other scholarship students from other drama schools. Other medallists, too."

"Belt up," Della commanded. "You're giving *me* nerves now — me, who can't even get within sniffing distance of an audition! As an actress I'll never make the grade, and well I know it."

"With your looks — "

"The only place *they*'ll get me to is the altar, with luck."

"Isn't that where we all want to get? You could do worse, you know."

"Sweetie, I do know. Trouble is, I never meet any males other than my father's tycoon friends, all very much married or very much divorced. Worse still, debs' delights looking for a wife to support them. The only alternatives are drama students — would-be actors, ducky, and you know what *they* are like. Half of them finish up as male models."

Susan laughed.

"Not all. Some make the grade."

"Like Stephen Hammond? Now there's a man I could fall for, and think, just *think* — if you land this part tomorrow you'll actually work with him!" Della sighed romantically. "He's the world's dreamiest male, and yet he leads such a blameless life! No breath of scandal ever touches him, and apart from the stage his name isn't even linked with Grace Challoner's!"

"Perhaps because she is happily married to someone else. It's common knowledge that she and Philip Dunster are madly happy together."

"I wonder how he feels, Philip Dunster, I mean, about his wife making love every night to the gorgeous Stephen."

"On stage only, so why should he worry?"

Della said passionately, "I do hope you land this part, then I'll be able to boast about sharing a flat with a member of the Comet Theatre Company! Maybe they'll sign you up on a long-term contract, like Ethel Fothergill and others."

"Well, I'm not counting my chickens.

I have to pass the hurdle of an audition first and the thought petrifies me." She yawned, shivering a little with excitement and dread. "I'm tired, but I know I won't sleep."

"Enough of that, my girl. Into bed with you and let Mother Della take over. You're having a nice cup of hot milk to lull you off. Isn't that what you said your mother used to give you at nights? I like the sound of your mum," Della continued, going into the two-by-four cupboard which served as a kitchen. "Now *my* mother's a sweetie, but she never brought me hot milk to bed in my life!"

Susan closed the window and drew the curtains against the night. It was no use lingering here, looking out on to a world which still clung to the day, where lights hung suspended in darkness like symbols of life. The minutes ticked by, bringing to-morrow remorselessly nearer. She feared it, dreaded it, and longed for it. I'll be paralysed, she thought. Paralysed right through. But she always was, always had been, right through school performances to the nerve-racking tests for the dramatic academy — and, once there, at every examination, every class rendering, every end-of-term show. But still she loved each tense and exciting moment of it, and the tension and excitement of to-morrow clutched at her now.

The last thing she saw before she drew the curtains was the hospital across the street. The ward windows were dimmed, but far below the lights of the casualty department spilled into the night. Distantly, she saw a man in a white coat walk towards an open window and pause briefly — a figure in black and white, indistinguishable from this distance, a doctor pausing in the midst of his work. Real work, real drama, she thought. Maybe Dad was right when he called the theatre 'this acting lark.'

But for her it was reality, life, the only thing she wanted to do. She was passionately serious about it and completely dedicated.

"If I don't get this part to-morrow," she called to Della, "I shall die a thousand deaths."

But Della merely called back, "Maybe you will, honey, but you'll come to life again a thousand times more, eager for another bash. Are you ready to drink this revolting stuff?"

4

MIDNIGHT, thought young Doctor Radcliffe, automatically setting his watch by Big Ben. Seven more hours before he went off casualty duty, and more than that before he could get along to the Comet Theatre to watch auditions for his play.

He still couldn't get over the miracle of it. Writing in a spate of concentrated fervour, passionate and intense, he had poured on to paper every emotion that had troubled and tortured him during the months of freedom which had proved to be no freedom at all. He had exorcised his bitterness, purged his mind of hatred, and emerged at the end of it feeling curiously light and free. The weight of heartsickness had gone, and with it his savage desire for revenge. He was calmed; a reasonable human being once more. As psychiatric treatment he couldn't have done anything better than to unload everything in this way and, as a doctor, he knew it. What he had not anticipated was the unexpected result of his effort. His play was accepted for production at the Comet Theatre within a month of submission.

He had expected the thing to boomerang back, and for this reason had forgotten about it the moment he sent it along — and he had only sent it because it was *there*, on his cluttered desk in his poky flat, a wedge of packed typescript demanding attention. Something had to be done with it. It had to go somewhere, even if it was only the back of a drawer.

On an impulse, after seeing the bundle lying there week after week, he had parcelled it up and despatched it to the Comet, and after that he gave his mind to work, his urge to be a playwright forgotten. Medicine absorbed him again.

Astonishment at having his play accepted was tinged with ironic humour, for acceptance came at a time when such success didn't really matter. He had got the play out of his system, and that was that. It was no longer necessary to prove that he could do it.

Nevertheless, being human, he felt

a little giddy with delight when the news came through, and the succeeding negotiations were exciting. He had also been allowed to attend auditions, a privilege not always granted to unknown authors, but right from the beginning Grace Challoner had been co-operative and kind. And now there was only one major part left to fill, that of Nina, the one character in the play who was truly a figment of his imagination.

But as he strolled across to a window in the casualty department, he wondered if that was really true. Perhaps Nina was the embodiment of everything he wanted to find in a woman and still believed could be found — a warm and feminine person with faults and weaknesses and virtues, a person capable of loving and of being loved, asking no more of life than to share it with someone equally human and emotional. What more simple and uncomplicated demand could anyone make of life, and what more difficult thing to find?

So Nina was important. In his mind's eye, he could see her — young and rather pensive, with straight dark hair falling in a curtain over one side of her face when she leaned forward, just as that girl at a faraway window leaned forward now. He had seen her before, although only at this moment did he recall the fact. Vaguely he had been aware that behind a distant window, several floors high across the street, the faces of two girls occasionally appeared — one red-headed and pert; the other less spectacular, with straight dark hair and an oval face. At this distance, the features of neither could be clearly distinguished, and as he glanced upwards the dark-haired girl, who had been leaning on the sill staring out into the night, suddenly closed the window and drew the curtains. "But I'd know her if we met," he thought unexpectedly, and closed his window, too, and went back to work.

At seven o'clock he went off duty. He snatched a couple of hours' sleep, wakened at nine, made some coffee, bathed, shaved, then indulged in the extravagance of a taxi to the theatre. He wasn't rich enough yet to take taxis as a matter of course, but maybe, if *Wings of Morning* were a hit, the day would come when he would do so, but he couldn't imagine it. He came from a large and struggling family in a less affluent part of South London and the squandering of seven and sixpence on what would have been a ninepenny bus ride was guaranteed to disturb his conscience.

That was the sort of reaction which, he knew from experience, could jar on a woman. Only someone from a similar background to his own would understand it; one accustomed to money would not. (*'You, a doctor, counting taxi fares? Really, David, you embarrass me!'*) As he paid off the taxi, adding a larger tip in defiance of his conscience, he could hear the words echoing clearly in his memory. Perhaps it was these words, and the voice that uttered them, that he really wanted to defy.

"I'm a doctor, yes, but still an unimportant one," he wanted to shout back. *'As yet.'*

Always, he was wanting to justify himself, but *why*, he wondered furiously as he walked down the alley leading to the Comet Theatre's stage door. That phase of his life was over, and the series of

35

scholarships which had led from grammar school to medical school were surely sufficient to prove that he was as good as, if not better than, many. And how had this stupid need for self-justification taken hold of him, anyway? At one time it had not been there. As a child and as a boy he had been uninhibited, self-confident, unaware of any social gaps in his background — then suddenly he was conscious of deficiencies and anxious to overcome them. Only on the wards, amongst the patients, did he truly forget himself now.

Standing in the wings backstage he was self-conscious and shy. None of the nurses who, unbeknown to him, whispered that he was the up-and-coming man at St. Bede's, would have recognised him, but this bleak and unfamiliar place lacked the comfort of the hospital and confidence deserted him. He felt annoyed with himself, because throughout night duty he had been looking forward to this morning; he refused to be cheated out of it by a stupid shyness now.

Tom Langley, the stage director, had already taken the iron safety curtain up and was shouting instructions from mid-stage to unseen hands above.

"Okay," he called. "Open up!"

With a great rush of air the heavy velvet tabs swooped apart, revealing an auditorium shrouded in dust-sheets and embalmed in the air of desolation peculiar to an empty theatre.

Stephen Hammond was there, standing by the orchestra rail — a man in his early forties, handsome, charming, debonair. He was popular and knew it — and loved it, David guessed. Sometimes on a ward there would be one particular patient who hogged the limelight, who was the nurses' favourite, who won the most sympathy, who attracted the most attention. Stephen Hammond would have been such a patient.

"Well," Stephen said, "we're in for a busy session. Candidates are queueing up already."

Old Tom Langley nodded his white head. "All the agencies in London must've got wind of it."

"Poor kids," said Stephen, his handsome face revealing kindly concern. "It's worse for them than for us. The doubt, the anxiety, the suspense — how well I remember going through it!"

It was one of his endearing qualities that despite his success he could always spare a thought for the underdog.

"How many on the list?" he asked Tom Langley.

"Well over eighty."

"And it's now a quarter to the hour. I suppose we couldn't begin early?"

"Grace isn't here. The call is for ten o'clock."

"Then I've time to read my mail."

Tom grinned.

"*All* of it, Stephen?"

As usual, the bundle of mail for Stephen Hammond was large. He gave a deprecatory smile, but really he loved it. Catching David's eye the smile flickered, and for a moment his expression became defensive. David was embarrassed and sorry. He had seen through the man's pretence, and Stephen knew it.

The actor suddenly stopped acting and said, "Frankly, Doctor, I'd worry if it didn't come. I count my letters every morning — by their number I stand, or fall. An actor's fan mail is the barometer of his success."

David smiled, understanding and sympathetic. When he smiled his serious face became unexpectedly attractive, the teeth very white and the curve of mouth warm and kind. He wasn't a handsome man, but people noticed him — especially women. His tall frame suggested strength and his eyes suggested courage and neither overrated him. He did have strength and he did have courage, and in the course of his life he had needed both.

"Come and join me, Doctor."

Stephen Hammond indicated the front row of the stalls, from which dust-sheets had been thrown back. As David walked through the iron pass door and emerged into the auditorium Stephen continued easily, "Let's drop the formalities, shall we? I can't call you Doctor for ever."

David smiled.

"There's nothing I'd like better."

Stephen Hammond put everyone at ease — even medical men accustomed to a very different type of theatre.

A moment later Grace appeared on-stage, carrying an armful of scripts.

These she handed over to Tom Langley, retaining one for herself. "Got yours, Stephen?" she called across the empty footlights. "What scene shall we take?"

She was brisk, businesslike, ready for work, glowing with vitality; a beautiful and confident young woman, filled with well-being.

"How about the scene where Nina comes downstairs after the death of her child — Act Two, Scene One? That's a test for any actress."

"Fine. The existing staircase can be used."

The stage was already set for the current production, which was due to be withdrawn in a fortnight. Meanwhile, casting auditions were held against the background of an Imperial palace in Ruritania.

Tom handed Grace a list on which were typed the names, addresses, training and experience of every applicant.

Grace glanced at it and suppressed a compassionate sigh. How could they all hope to make the grade in an already over-crowded profession? As each one stepped on to the stage she would feel the familiar sympathy and irritation, the desire to say, "Go home, child, and take up something else. Don't waste your precious youth chasing rainbows. Success is for the few — the rare and the talented, or the ruthless and unscrupulous. If you are not the former, don't stay in this profession and become the latter!"

But one didn't say it; one couldn't. One smiled and said politely, "Thank you. We will let you know," and fidgeted in one's seat and braced oneself for the next uninspired performance. Except when, like a breath of revitalising air, talent suddenly leapt across the empty footlights, bringing a desolate theatre gloriously to life.

She walked through the pass door and took her place beside David and Stephen. "All right," she said. "Let's go."

And so it began, the endless parade of hopefuls. By noon not one young actress came anywhere near David's conception of Nina. Beside him Grace suppressed a yawn and Stephen, muttering an excuse, left the stalls and went backstage. For the past hour he had become increasingly fidgety, and this sign of

41

nerves caught David's attention. Nerves were out of keeping with the public image of Stephen Hammond, which was one of a man supremely confident, debonair, and smiling. Nerves were symptomatic, and the symptoms David detected now were disturbing.

He watched the actor's abrupt departure with concern, but Grace merely watched with annoyance. These tensed-up moods of Stephen's were becoming more and more frequent.

"Thank you, my dear, that will do," she called politely to the girl on-stage, and another young hopeful passed into the wings.

Tom Langley called the next name, and a girl entered with quick, light steps. David looked at her and looked again. She was young, slim, with beautiful legs and straight dark hair falling to her shoulders. When the stage director handed her the script she bent her head to study it and her hair swept forward in a shining curtain which she brushed aside with impatient, sensitive fingers.

Her face was oval, delicately formed and vaguely familiar. At first, David thought this was because she came so near to his visual idea of Nina, and then he suddenly remembered where he had seen her. *I would know her if we met*, he had thought as he closed the window in Casualty last night.

He was conscious of a quickening interest, tinged with surprise.

"Susan Howard . . . scholarship student . . . bronze medallist," Grace read aloud from her list. "So this is the girl Stephen was so impressed with. She should be good."

She was. From the moment that Tom Langley began reading with her, she grasped the feeling of the lines with a sure touch, and the atmosphere in the theatre became suddenly revitalised. Grace leaned forward, arms resting on the seat in front, and her excitement communicated itself to David.

"After raving about this girl ever since he saw her in a RADA performance, Stephen disappears when it's her turn to be auditioned!" Grace muttered impatiently. "Where can he have got to?"

It was at that precise moment that

the noise occurred off-stage, shattering the magic like a burst bubble. Susan jerked to attention, nerves jangled and concentration broken.

Grace called out sharply, "What was that? Who made that noise? What's going on back there?"

There were suppressed giggles from the girls waiting in the wings, and Tom Langley, after glancing off-stage, walked down to the footlights and said, "It's all right, Grace — it's only Stephen. He tripped on the spiral staircase."

"What is he *doing* on the spiral staircase?" Grace answered with amused impatience.

"Been to his dressing-room, I suppose," Tom said, and Stephen walked on-stage, full of penitent charm.

"Darling," he called to Grace, "forgive the interruption. If this theatre weren't so damned old-fashioned it would have decent stairs instead of that antiquated iron thing. It's a danger to life and limb."

He was himself again, smiling and debonair, the charm switched on full current. Now he turned to Susan,

44

standing there clutching her script like an unnerved child. "My dear, forgive me. You were doing so well, too, as I knew you would. I recognised your voice as I came downstairs. Don't let this interruption upset you. Start again, please." With all the theatricality of the born actor he kissed her cheek with a flourish. "There — am I forgiven?"

"Of course," Susan stammered, her heart warming to him.

Waiting for Stephen to reach his seat in the stalls again gave her a chance to compose herself. The little fracas off-stage had unnerved her at a moment when any interruption was as discordant as a wrongly struck note.

Tom Langley gave her an encouraging smile.

"Don't worry, dear. Take your time," he said, and Grace called, "Would you mind starting the scene again, Miss Howard? You're good. Very good."

Susan was grateful. Grace Challoner was endeavouring to put her at ease again. As Susan took up her position, Grace said to Stephen, "Did you *have* to go to your dressing-room? Why, for heaven's sake? To answer some adoring fan letter?"

"Why not?" muttered Stephen.

Susan looked beyond the proscenium arch and saw that Stephen Hammond had settled himself beside Grace and another man. Vaguely, she wondered who he was, but dismissed him and turned her attention back to the audition.

"I saw some flowers off-stage," she said. "May I use them? I see from the script that Nina is carrying flowers on her entrance."

"Of course, my dear. Use any props you like."

Tom Langley fetched them and the scene began again with Susan descending the Ruritanian staircase, carrying the sheaf of flowers as if she were carrying a child. "*These were the flowers she loved* . . . " she said, and into the listening silence the words fell like drops of water, crystal clear. Even the blasé theatre staff paused to listen.

Occasionally, just occasionally, it was like this. A hundred or more trooped across the stage and said lines and did their stuff, but they weren't worth

46

stopping the dusting for; you could listen to 'em and go right on sweeping up last night's chocolate wrappings. And then someone appeared — sometimes a man, sometimes a woman, sometimes young, sometimes old — and everyone in the theatre knew, from the producer down to the stage hands, from the stage hands to the cleaners, that they were in the presence of talent. Real talent, such as this girl had.

There was an instant of complete silence when she finished, then Stephen Hammond said, "Didn't I tell you she was good? You'll sign her up, of course."

"Of course," Grace agreed. To Susan, she called, "Thank you, Miss Howard. Will you wait, please?"

David said nothing. He just sat there, aware of an intense excitement. When Grace turned to him and said, "She's Nina to the life, isn't she?" he nodded mutely. She had come alive before him, the girl of his dreams.

Susan walked towards the prompt corner. There was a young woman waiting there, but she scarcely noticed her, nor paused to wonder why the next candidate had stationed herself at the wrong side. Auditioners were lined up at the off-prompt corner, but when the next candidate was called the girl who was standing alone hurried forward, taking the stage with determination. Susan paid her no heed. Tension had relaxed in her like an unwound spring, and now relief mixed with a kind of incredulous excitement possessed her. She had been told to wait. That meant a lot.

She sat down at the foot of the spiral staircase. As Stephen Hammond had said, the Comet was an old-fashioned place, and it was a long time since theatres had been built with an ancient iron staircase spiralling upwards to unseen dressing-rooms above. The steps were grilled and the outside was flanked by a single banister rail. The inner side, quite unprotected, curved round a central well. It was more like a twisting iron ladder than a staircase.

"An actor 'anged 'imself from that banister rail way back in the eighteen 'undreds," said a stage hand beside her, "and once, after a first-night party back-stage, another fell down the centre well and broke 'is neck. A drop too much, if you asks me."

Susan shuddered, and the man grinned. "Shouldn't let it worry you, m'dear. Nothink like that's likely to 'appen to you. Congratulations, miss. You've done it, I'm sure. Stage staff can always tell. I'll bet me bottom dollar the part's yours."

5

WHEN Maxine walked on stage she was aware of the impact she made, and was pleased. She was an arresting type, and knew it, but she also knew that it was more than her looks that focused attention now. She stationed herself in the centre, down stage, and smiled into the auditorium, seeing David's face staring at her in astonishment. She hoped he was as stunned as he looked.

She was aware that on the off-prompt side an altercation was taking place. The girl she had superceded was protesting, and Maxine acted swiftly to forestall her. She picked up a script from the stage director's table, saying as she did so, "Hello, Tom. Remember me? We toured together once upon a time."

Tom Langley, surprised and disconcerted, answered, "Sorry, Maxine — I didn't realise — "

"That's all right. Let's get on with it, shall we?"

But Tom was puzzled. He studied the call list in his hand, then said into the auditorium, "I'm afraid there's been a slip-up somewhere. Miss Culver's name isn't on my list. Is she on yours, Grace?"

"Sorry, Tom, I should have let you know. Late last night I agreed to her having an audition, but I did say she would have to be the last."

With a disarming smile Maxine pleaded, "Would you be *terribly* kind and hear me now? My agent wants me to see a casting director in Wardour Street later, and if I wait until last I'll miss the appointment. I hate filming, but what actress can afford to miss a chance?"

Fine, thought Grace. That's a perfect let-out for us. She was about to agree when Stephen said, "Whoever she is, she'll have to wait her turn. And why didn't you let *me* know, Grace?"

Before Grace had a chance to answer a voice spoke from behind.

"There wasn't time. I didn't ring Grace until midnight. She promised to give Maxine an audition as a favour to me. The girl is my niece."

51

They turned and saw Ethel Fothergill sitting behind. She looked tired, Stephen thought, as if she had had a sleepless night, so he said kindly, "That's all right, dear, although we make it a rule not to add to the call list once it is closed, but in this case . . . "

Grace said in some concern, "Ethel dear, what are you doing here?" She wanted to point out that it was her job to do the casting, with Stephen to comment and advise, and that ordinary members of the company had no right to be present at auditions, but Ethel's anxiety communicated like a dark and compelling undercurrent, so Grace said no more.

"All right," Stephen called to Maxine. "You may take your turn now."

Maxine smiled with touching gratitude, and launched straight into her performance. Experience had taught her to memorise lines, and after listening to a succession of applicants reading them it was scarcely necessary to glance at the script. Even more skilfully she memorised Susan Howard's moves, reproducing them with almost mechanical precision.

Grace said to David, "She's modelling her performance on the previous girl's. That's a mistake. She should give us her own interpretation."

But Maxine couldn't possibly interpret the part, not as he had created it, David thought. Nina was a girl he had dreamed up in direct contrast to Maxine herself; a girl to replace her in his memory. To him, there was bitter irony in her attempt to become that girl, and now he had recovered from the shock of seeing her, he felt almost amused.

Stephen remarked, "Technically, her performance cannot be faulted; emotionally, it is lacking. We've seen enough of her, don't you think?"

Grace agreed, and chanted the age-old words of dismissal. "Thank you, Miss Culver. We'll let you know."

David suppressed a sigh of relief. He wanted nothing so much as to see Maxine walk off that stage and out of his life again, this time for ever.

Arrested in the middle of speech, Maxine stared across the footlights in astonishment. Her audition had lasted no time at all; she was dismissed peremptorily, and yet that chit of a girl straight out of drama school had been allowed to perform the whole scene. *And* been asked to wait at the end of it.

Anger took possession of her, but with magnificent control she thrust it back. *I can wait*, she thought. *I can bide my time*. She gave a charming smile and walked off into the wings.

Ethel Fothergill said anxiously, "Well?"

"I'm sorry, Ethel. You could see for yourself that she's wrong for the part."

"It would come! With rehearsals, it would come."

"Not a hope," said Stephen Hammond. "Besides, *I* want Susan Howard. We'll have to audition the rest, of course, but it would take someone brilliant to beat that girl and brilliance doesn't come along twice in one day. Time for lunch, I think." He called to Langley, "Tell the rest to come back in an hour's time," and made his way to the pass door with David Radcliffe, leaving the two women alone.

Ethel slumped in her seat and Grace said in concern, "Ethel, dear, don't take it like that. We did our best for her. She can't blame you for her failure."

"You don't understand," the older woman answered dully. "You just don't understand. You'll have to engage her. You won't have any choice."

"But that's nonsense — "

Ethel didn't listen. She rose wearily and followed the two men. Impulsively, Grace called after her, "If it will make you any happier, we'll give her the under-study."

Ethel looked back, a wry smile touching her lips.

"I doubt if she'd take it. Maxine considers herself above that."

But still Grace was anxious to comfort her old friend.

"Perhaps she'll land the film part her agent has lined up."

This time Ethel's smile was even more wry. She had recognised that story as a bit of sales talk on Maxine's part. Only last night she had admitted that she had quarrelled with her agent, and that no other in London would handle her.

"Come and have a bite in my dressing-room," Grace invited, but Ethel shook her head. She wanted to go home, back to her little flat by the river. She wanted to be alone, and if Maxine called, furious and threatening, she wouldn't answer. She knew that her niece would not accept rejection. She wanted the part, and she would get it, no matter how.

Grace kissed Ethel's cheek impulsively. "Put your feet up and have a good rest before the performance to-night. You'll feel better then." She wanted to ask the woman what was troubling her, but refrained. If it concerned Maxine, she didn't really want to know.

Turning to her dressing-room, which led immediately off the wings beside the spiral staircase, she came face to face with Tom Langley.

"Shall I have a tray sent over for you?" he asked.

Opposite the stage door was an obliging Italian restaurant.

"Something light," Grace told him. "And when it comes, will you see that I'm not disturbed? I'd like half an hour's rest before we start again."

He smiled with understanding. "Leave it to me," he said, and her heart warmed to him. Dear old Daddy Langley, father to everyone in the company; a lovable man, with guileless eyes.

Crossing back stage, she saw Susan Howard sitting at the foot of the spiral staircase and went to her, holding out her hand.

"Congratulations, Susan. Your performance was very promising. We'll want to have a talk with you when all auditions are through. Can you come back?"

"I'd rather wait," Susan said breathlessly.

"Then don't do it on an empty stomach," Grace advised with a smile.

"She's not going to. She's coming with me." David Radcliffe was beside them. "I'll bring her back, don't worry. We're not going to lose her."

Grace smiled as she watched them depart, amused by Susan's surprise and David's determination. She had judged him to be a quiet, unassuming, over-serious young man. Apparently he could be masterful, too.

"Anyway," David continued as he led Susan away, "we're practically next-door neighbours, so that gives me certain rights."

"Does it? Are we?" she stammered.

"Hailing neighbours, as you might say. Not over the garden wall, but across the street, except that you're several floors above me — when I'm on duty, that is. Off duty, I live a couple of blocks away — handy for the hospital, and cheap. Both are considerations in a lesser physician's life."

"You're a doctor, then? Funny — I thought you must be something to do with the play."

"Merely the author."

Susan regarded him with awe.

"A fluke," he said quickly. "I'll probably never write another."

They had reached the stage door and stepped out into the street. David hailed a taxi and gave the address of a nearby restaurant.

Susan gasped, "A taxi — just for *that* short trip? We could walk it!"

"But this is a celebration. We must do the thing in style."

"A celebration for what?"

"For getting the part."

"Then I really have got it?" she breathed.

"That's obvious, although it's not for

me to tell you. Didn't Grace Challoner say anything?"

"Only that we were to have a talk."

"There you are, then! Surely you guessed?"

"I didn't dare!"

She closed her eyes in brief ecstasy, then opened them wide. They were large, smoky-blue, and long-lashed. She was awfully young, he thought, with a sudden rush of emotion that he interpreted as compassion.

She said with a touch of awe, "Fancy being a doctor as well as a playwright . . . "

"Let's say a playwright as well as a doctor — there's a subtle distinction."

"Meaning that you're a doctor first?"

"First, and last."

"But you'll write more plays?"

"I don't know. Perhaps. This was just something I had to get off my chest."

She didn't ask why, and he was glad.

"I hope I can do justice to the part," she said anxiously. "I hope I interpret it the way you imagined."

"I don't think you need worry on that score."

The taxi drew to a halt and he didn't spare the meter a glance, thrusting a note into the driver's hand. His conscience didn't even stir. It was cheap at the price, he thought. *Walk?* On a red-letter day like this?

6

OPENING the door of her dressing-room, Grace Challoner stood still abruptly. With her hand still on the knob, she said coldly. "May I ask what you are doing here?"

Maxine, lolling in the one and only easy-chair, smiled insolently and replied, "Certainly. I'm waiting for you, Mrs. Martinelli."

Grace went rigid. She felt sick. The pit of her stomach contracted as if a cold hand had clutched it.

She closed the door and walked slowly across the room.

"I don't know what you are talking about."

Maxine laughed.

"Oh, yes, you do, Mrs. Martinelli."

"My name is Dunster. I am Mrs. Philip Dunster."

"You're not. You married Luigi Martinelli in Australia when you were seventeen — a bit young, I admit, but old enough to know what you were doing." She opened her handbag and took out a folded newspaper cutting. "Don't deny it. I have proof."

Grace sat down before her dressing-table. She sat abruptly, her legs betraying her. She surveyed Maxine through the mirror, hating her as she had never hated anyone before. She wanted to order her from the room. She wanted to open the dressing-room door and call Tom Langley to throw the girl out. She wanted to hit that insolent face and go right on hitting it. The primitiveness of her reaction shocked her deeply.

Taking a steadying breath she answered, "I don't know where you dug up this information, but let's get it straight, shall we? I married a man named Lew Martin many years ago — as you say, when I was seventeen. He died two and a half years later and after that I married Philip Dunster. I am his legal wife."

"Not if your first husband turns up, and you were never divorced. That makes you a bigamist."

The knuckles of Grace's hands, clenched in her lap, showed white. Maxine's eyes flickered to them, and away again.

"I told you — Lew Martin is dead. I was a widow when I met and married my present husband."

"Sorry to disappoint you, but you were never a widow. Luigi Martinelli — alias Lew Martin — was sentenced in Australia to twenty years for robbery with violence, plus other crimes. He was sent to Long Bay Jail, in Sydney, with two of his colleagues — Carl Jonsen and Pete Riddle."

"And there he died. I was notified."

"Do you still have that notification?"

She hadn't. She had destroyed it, along with every other reminder, wiping out the past, starting a new life.

"*If* they did," Maxine said sceptically, "they made a mistake, but there can be no mistake about this. The three of them have escaped. It's all here, plus a photograph of your wedding, which the other two men attended. You remember them, I'm sure. It's a charming group, isn't it? Looking at Luigi in his immaculate clothes one would never suspect him of being a criminal." Maxine studied the newspaper photograph with an amused smile. "And the bride looks so innocent, doesn't she? Apart from ageing somewhat, you haven't really changed. It's easily recognisable as you. So is the photograph of my aunt — also at the wedding. What a pretty little story to have hushed up all these years. But how is it going to be hushed up now?"

"Let me see that."

"Certainly." Maxine handed it over. "See the headline? Fancy making a break for it after serving so much of his sentence. Hardly worth while, I should have thought. Only a few years to go, and they would have been reduced had he behaved himself."

But Grace wasn't listening. She was staring into her past, emphasised by the naked headline.

'*Long-term prisoners escape. Daring break by the three men from Long Bay Jail.*' And beneath, the caption read, '*The photograph shows Luigi Martinelli on the occasion of his marriage. Carl Jonsen and Pete Riddle stand one on each side of the bride and groom. The three men were sentenced six months later.*'

"Where is the rest of it?" Grace demanded. "There must have been more than this. An editorial report of some kind . . . "

"Of course. I have it. That's my insurance."

"Your — insurance?"

"I anticipated that you might do precisely what you are doing now — tearing it up. It makes no difference — I have all the details. The report, of course, gives the name of the bride, as well."

Grace looked down at her hands. Fragments of the *Sydney Morning Herald* stared up at her. With a hopeless gesture she threw them in an ashtray and set light to them. Maxine watched with an indifferent smile.

"How did you get hold of it?" Grace asked wretchedly.

"By the merest luck. The bartender at a little drinking club I go to happens to be Australian and his folks back home send him the local papers from time to time. When he has read them, he leaves them around. They're always a week or two old, of course. Martinelli and his cronies could be on their way to England by now."

"What are you leading up to?" Grace asked tensely. She was trembling and couldn't hide it.

"Can't you guess? Give me the part of Nina and I'll keep my mouth shut. I'll destroy the rest of the cutting, too, and you can watch me do it. If you don't agree — " she shrugged. "Does your husband know about Luigi?"

"He knows I have been married before. Naturally, I told him. He knows I was a widow. I told him that, too."

"And his family? What of them?"

The Dunsters. That respectable and respected family. And Philip, in his position of trust — what of him? Public exposure of his wife as an accessory who had luckily been acquitted could do him untold harm.

Grace closed her eyes, feeling the edifice of her secure and happy world rocking perilously. She had told Philip what she had considered to be enough, but no more, because all those years ago she had been desperately afraid of losing him. She had never loved any man so much in all her life, and never would again. Was silence, or a half-silence, too great a price to pay for happiness? She hadn't thought so at the time, although there had been moments since when she had wished that she had told him everything down to the last sordid detail.

But, as always in those days, she had turned to Ethel for advice, and until now it had seemed sound advice. Grace could hear the older woman's words echoing in her ears quite plainly.

"Least said the better, dear. Lew Martin or Luigi Martinelli, or whatever else he called himself, is dead. He belongs to the past and cannot touch you."

But now she learned that he could — and through this girl. Maxine had only to walk out of the theatre and down to Fleet Street to expose the unsavoury story, and by morning the whole country would know it. And Maxine wasn't a girl to have qualms about hurting or even destroying someone.

Grace looked at her for a long moment, then said slowly, *"I could kill you for this."*

7

ACROSS Maxine's shoulder, Grace saw Tom Langley standing in the doorway.

"I knocked," he said. "I knocked twice."

Grace pulled herself together.

"I'm sorry, Tom, I didn't hear you."

But *he* had heard *her*. She was sure of that. Even now her words seemed to echo in the narrow room — ugly, menacing, and determined.

"They're rushed off their feet over at the Trattoria, so I brought you coffee and sandwiches. Will that do?"

She was glad of the coffee, but had no appetite for the sandwiches.

Tom said, "Believe it or not, the ever-hopefuls are trooping back already, waiting in the wings to be auditioned."

Maxine laughed.

"Poor things. What a waste of time!"

Tom looked at her, puzzled. Then he looked at Grace. It seemed to him that

68

she deliberately avoided his eyes, and the action was so unusual that he was disturbed. He looked back at Maxine, disliking her. But he had always disliked her, ever since that unhappy tour of the provinces from which he had been abruptly sacked. He had never been sure, but had always felt that this girl was responsible. He had been road manager for the show, and one evening had caught her in the dressing-room which served as his office. She had explained her presence easily enough ('I came to borrow a stamp, darling — the post office is closed at this hour'), but he had been uneasy, and not without cause. The drawer in which he kept the company's share of the box office receipts had been open, and one glance would have told anyone that for a show that was doing singularly well the till was short.

That was why he always kept it locked, but the lock had been a common type, easily opened with a common type of key. A practised swindler would have remedied that, but he wasn't practised — just stupid, thoughtless, blindly reckless, for after a long spell of unemployment Sylvia's final illness had begun and he had determined that the wife he adored should have the best specialists, the best treatment, no matter what the cost.

A temporary borrowing had been an act of desperation bitterly paid for. In a short time he could have replaced it, but suddenly it was discovered and he was dismissed. There had been no official charge, no exposure; he had been given the chance to make repayment, but never again could he get a road manager's job, and even now the fear of meeting anyone who remembered his one tragic lapse made him break out in a cold sweat. If the story came out it could do him untold harm again. He was too old now to make a fresh start.

Thank God, Sylvia had never known about that terrible business. She died shortly after, despite all efforts to save her. Even his desperate attempt to give her nothing but the best had been a waste of time.

He turned away from Maxine's smiling face, refusing to believe that behind it he saw any taunting reminder. It had all happened long ago. Surely she didn't remember? The whole thing had been hushed up by a sympathetic management and he didn't know whether any member of the company had been aware of the reason for his sudden departure.

Grace said abruptly, "Let's get on with the auditions, shall we? If Stephen isn't back, we can start without him."

As she walked out of the dressing-room, Tom saw that she looked white and strained. He felt concern, because he was devoted to her and owed her a lot. Some months after his wife's death, when he had lost all interest in life, Grace had traced him to a dreary room in Brixton. Once upon a time Sylvia had put a job in her way, and Grace had never forgotten. When she saw Tom's reduced circumstances she packed his few belongings, dismissed all protests and took him home with her. Philip Dunster hadn't turned a hair, although what the classy relatives who dined there that night thought of his wife's slightly seedy friend Tom could well imagine.

For a month the Dunsters housed him until a room which Grace thought good enough for him was found. Then he started work at the Comet and never looked back. Now he was content, happy in his job of stage director, financially comfortable, and far from seedy.

So the arrival of this girl, like an unhappy shadow from the past, was a reminder he didn't welcome.

He was surprised to find her in Grace's dressing-room, because her audition had been unsuccessful, slick and professional as it was. They had found the girl they wanted, so he couldn't understand why Grace had sent for Maxine.

Grace felt ten years older as she made her way back to the stalls. On the way she met Susan, returning from lunch. She was alone, but starry-eyed. Grace turned away quickly. I can't look her in the face, she thought wretchedly. I can't look any of them in the face, except Ethel.

Suddenly, she felt a need to talk to Ethel, but the woman had gone.

Now she knew what Ethel meant when she said that there 'would be no choice.' Maxine had not been blackmailing her aunt; she had been blackmailing Grace *through* her aunt. But Ethel was involved.

She knew all about the unhappy past because she had been a close spectator and she had everything to lose if the story ruined the Comet Theatre Company, so no wonder she had been anxious.

Ethel had been there when Lew and Grace met during that long-ago tour of Australia — the first job Grace had ever had. Ethel had watched with maternal benevolence while the dashing young man from Melbourne gave the girl a rush, sweeping her into a register office on a romantic tide. By then they had known each other only a month, and six months later the end had come with all its hideous disillusion and shock.

The starry-eyed young bride had believed her husband to be a wealthy young Australian play-boy whom marriage would sober. Instead, he proved to be one of the most unscrupulous racketeers ever to emigrate to that continent from Naples. His accent had been explained by an upbringing with an Italian aunt, and, of course, the seventeen-year-old Grace had believed him. Why shouldn't she? Why shouldn't she believe that the jewels he lavished upon her were bought with his own money? But at the trial it had been hard to convince the judge that she had been an unsuspecting pawn, the unwitting recipient of stolen property.

Lew had been clever — she had to hand him that. He had seen what an asset a young and ignorant wife could be, accepting gifts from her husband without question, putting them in a safe deposit on his advice — in her own name, of course. Fortunately, the jury had believed her story, or perhaps her youth had convinced them. At seventeen she had been naïve and trusting to a degree, and in view of the fact that many older and wiser people had been taken in by Lew Martin, this had swung the balance in her favour. But even now the horror and uncertainty of the trial could return to her in nightmares, and this was the worst nightmare of all.

She thought, I must play for time, and I must talk to Philip. I'll have to tell him everything.

The thought wasn't pleasant, but she wasn't afraid. Ten years of happy marriage had inspired a mutual trust between them. What she *did* fear was adverse publicity for him. For herself, it didn't matter so much; actresses could survive an awful lot of bad publicity and even be glamorised by it, but if the newspapers got wind of an ugly story about his wife they could bespatter Philip with it. His position didn't make him impregnable, but vulnerable. The story would be devoured by an avid public and made capital out of by his political enemies.

So, at all costs, he had to be armed with the truth, otherwise it could take him unawares, before he had time to decide how to cope with it. All she had told him of her previous marriage was that it had been contracted when she was too young to have any sense, with a man who was no good at all and had ultimately died in prison, which she believed to be true.

In order to gain time now she had no choice but to string along with Maxine, otherwise the girl would be quite unscrupulous. If she would stoop to blackmail to get herself a part in a new London production, she would stoop to anything. So, for the time being, it was essential to string along — but only for the time being.

I'll get Philip to deal with her, Grace resolved. He will know what to do.

As always, she had absolute confidence in her husband's wisdom and judgment, but this didn't stop her from feeling sick and frightened. As she sat in the stalls, trying to concentrate on the remaining auditions, the terrifying possibility of Lew returning from the dead, and announcing to all the world that she was still his lawful wedded wife, became a suffocating terror in her heart.

She was scarcely aware of Stephen's arrival. He was buoyant and gay, his morning irritation vanished, dismissing girl after girl with his unique brand of charm so that even failure seemed almost worth while to them. "Darling, you are absolutely charming and I'm sure you'll go right to the top one day, but for this play — not *quite* right, dear. But thank you for coming." And with a dazzling and endearing smile, he speeded them on their way.

When at last the auditions were over, he sat back, glanced at his watch and gave a prodigious yawn.

"A quarter to six — well, thank heaven it's all over. Now we can sign up Susan Howard."

Grace took a deep breath. "I'm sorry. I don't agree."

He stared at her. "What in heaven's name do you mean?"

"She is too inexperienced. I'll engage her as understudy."

"And who, pray, is to have the part? Or shouldn't I ask?"

He was always most difficult to handle when in a sarcastic mood.

"Ethel's niece, Maxine Culver."

The transitions from gaiety to sarcasm to blazing temper could be achieved by Stephen in a flash, and he achieved them now. All his good humour was switched off like a light. Grace had seen this happen before when he didn't get his own way, and his variable moods had become worse of late. During the past twelve months he had grown more and more unpredictable. At one moment he would be morose and nerve-ridden, his face taking on a peculiar palor which Grace found alarming, and then, a short time later, he would be himself again, his colour back, his eyes bright, his whole personality changed.

Only when acting was he really reliable, because he automatically projected himself into a part the moment he went on-stage. His talent was superb and she could not have asked for a better leading man, but there had been moments recently when she wondered whether she had been wise in seeking his advice so often, for now he assumed that she couldn't do without it and that he had every right to share decisions.

"What has come over you?" he demanded furiously. "This morning you were delighted with Susan. You said yourself that no one else could compare with her and you didn't want Ethel's niece at any price. What has happened to make you change your mind?"

"Nothing. I have merely thought things over and decided that we should engage someone more experienced. Susan has only just graduated from drama school. So she can have the under-study. My mind is made up."

"And so is mine!" Stephen stormed.

"You'll ruin the play if you put that Culver girl in it, so either she goes or I do!"

"I'm sorry you feel like that about it," Grace said calmly.

She picked up her bag and walked away from him. He watched her, stunned, then hurried after her.

"Do you actually mean you would *let* me go?" He was as hurt as a spoilt boy.

"Oh, Stephen, do grow up. Stop using threats when you can't get your own way. As for ruining the play," she finished tactfully, "how could it possibly flop with you in the lead?"

She realised at that moment how continuously she had to resort to flattery in her dealings with Stephen. All the same, what she said was true. A series of popular films had established his public image so successfully that people flocked to see whatever he was in, and they were never disappointed. He was a big box-office draw, and both of them knew it. Were he to leave, receipts would undoubtedly drop, so he had power to a certain extent. Nevertheless, she was determined not to yield. She couldn't afford to.

"Let me have my own way over this," she said persuasively. "If Maxine isn't successful at rehearsals, I'll think again, but let's give her a fair trial."

That would, at least, give Philip time to silence the girl's threats.

Stephen's stormy reaction had subsided a little, but he sulked as they went backstage. Maxine watched their approach with a self-satisfied smile, lolling up against the door of the star dressing-room as if she owned it. I can't stand the girl, Stephen thought ferociously, aware that in an obscure way he was afraid of her. He had noticed her this morning when he had sought brief refuge in his dressing-room. It was one of his bad moments and when the attacks came on it was hard to hide the symptoms. Brushing past the girl as he reached the spiral staircase he had seen her glance — sharp, assessing, knowledgeable — and for one sickening moment had felt that she realised what was wrong. But that was ridiculous, of course. Nevertheless, he resented that searching glance and took an instinctive dislike to her. When she was dismissed after her audition he felt relief that she would not be in the company. She was a stranger to him, and he wanted her to remain that way. He didn't like people who saw too much.

Susan Howard was standing aside, waiting with the suppressed excitement of a schoolgirl who knows she has won top prize. Grace's heart stabbed. She was going to hurt this girl, but a choice between hurting her and hurting Philip presented only one solution.

"Where is Doctor Radcliffe?" Grace asked her.

"He had to report for duty at the hospital at three."

Susan was sorry he wouldn't be there when she officially heard the news, but he had drunk to her success, raising his glass to her across the lunch table.

"When I thought up the part of Nina," he had said, "I must have had you in mind."

The lunch had been a gay little celebration, and she couldn't get home fast enough to tell Della that she had landed the part, although she knew exactly what Della would say — "Didn't I *tell* you so?"

Stephen Hammond said, "I'm sorry David isn't here. He would have been my ally."

Susan didn't know what he meant and scarcely paid any attention; she waited breathlessly for Grace Challoner to speak, and couldn't understand why the woman seemed unable to. It was almost as if she avoided her eye, and when Stephen said goadingly, "Go on, darling, tell the poor child and get it over," an alarming premonition ran through Susan, like a cold shiver.

Maxine Culver strolled across; smiling, charming, friendly. "I assume you are to be my under-study?" she said. "I'd like to be the first to congratulate you. An under-study at the Comet is quite a plum for a newly-fledged drama student to pull out of the pie."

Grace said sharply, "It is for me to tell her, not you."

But now, of course, it wasn't necessary. Susan was standing very still and her face paled. Grace put out a hand and said, "I'm sorry, my dear. Forgive me if I raised your hopes . . . " but the girl's silence made her voice tail away unhappily.

What a ghastly mistake to have made, Susan thought numbly, and how had it happened? But it hadn't been solely her mistake. David Radcliffe had told her the part was hers. That, he said, was what Grace Challoner wanted to talk to her about. He would be equally shocked when he heard how wrong he was.

Somehow, Susan smiled. She felt her lips move stiffly and hoped no one would guess how sick with disappointment she felt.

"Thank you, Miss Challoner. I'm pleased . . . proud . . . to be chosen as under-study."

At least she said the right thing and hoped it sounded convincing, but she couldn't get away fast enough.

"May I — go now?" she stammered.

"Of course, my dear. Report at eleven to-morrow morning — your contract will be ready then. Rehearsals for the principals start at once, and you will have to attend every one. Under-study rehearsals, commence later, by which time you will know all the lines and all the moves . . . "

Again, Grace's voice faltered. She was horribly aware of the girl's disappointment and the valiant effort she made to hide it. Grace added impulsively, "I'm sorry, Susan, deeply sorry, but I hope we'll be able to make it up to you in our next production."

"I should damn well hope so!" Stephen burst out. He put a commiserating arm about Susan's shoulders. "I'm going to buy you a good stiff drink, my dear. Doctor's orders. And I'm quite sure that if David Radcliffe were here he would need one, too. Brandy, for shock."

Grace turned away, not sparing a glance for Maxine. The door leading from the stage to the street closed behind her. Stephen was about to open it again when Maxine's voice arrested him.

She said, "I shouldn't be too sure of that, Mr. Hammond."

He turned, and Susan with him. "What do you mean?" he asked.

"That it won't be a shock to David." Stephen's handsome brow creased in

84

a puzzled frown. "I don't understand," he said.

Susan didn't understand, either.

"It's perfectly simple," Maxine explained. "Far from being a shock to him, it will be a pleasant surprise. What author wouldn't be pleased to hear that his wife was to appear in his own play?"

8

THIS time the whole back-stage area seemed to rock. Susan put out a hand and grasped one of the supporting stays of the scenery. She badly needed a prop herself; two unpleasant shocks within minutes of each other were more than the average person could be expected to take after a day of tension.

She heard Stephen say slowly, "So *that*'s it. Now I see how the whole thing happened. I must say Radcliffe's a dark horse, sitting there in the stalls this morning, not saying a word, agreeing whole-heartedly when we said that Susan was the girl for the part, coming back-stage and carrying her off to lunch while *you*, his wife, went to work on dear Grace behind everyone's back!" He walked across to Maxine and stood looking down at her with an expression of detached curiosity. "This time yesterday I didn't even know you existed. David has never mentioned you. Come to think of it, he's never even mentioned that he had a wife. And then suddenly you're in — lined up for an audition because your aunt pulled the necessary strings. How did you go to work on *her*, may I ask? Bully her into it? Or did that nice husband of yours persuade her? Perhaps he took *her* out to lunch, too? As a family I must say your methods of getting your own way are pretty thorough. Congratulate David for me, will you?"

He took hold of Susan's arm and marched her away. She was only too glad, for suddenly she felt that she was going to cry, and to do so before David's wife would be a final humiliation.

They had reached the door when Maxine called, "Wait!" When Stephen took no notice she hurried across. "Please don't go like that. Since we are to act together don't you think we should be friends?" Her voice was gentle and persuasive, very hard to resist. "Don't let's start off on the wrong foot," she begged.

"We've already done so," Stephen snapped.

"Then I'd like to put it right. I'd like to make amends."

"Make amends!" he exploded. "Then you do admit you've something to make amends *for*?" He looked at Susan, aware that behind the wan mask of her face tears hovered perilously. Then he looked back at Maxine. "There's only one thing I would like to do," he declared. "I'd like to wring your beautiful neck."

That was a mistake, and the minute he had spoken, he knew it. Something flickered in Maxine's eyes — a touch of flint, a sting, a poisoned arrow of hatred. She wouldn't forgive him for that; she was too accustomed to male susceptibility and, when she chose to assert her charm, expected them to come to heel. She looked at Stephen for a long moment, then shrugged and turned away, but suddenly he remembered that betraying moment at the foot of the spiral staircase, and her too-knowledgeable glance. Silently, she had reminded him of it now, and his confidence was shaken.

But after threatening to wring someone's

neck you could hardly extend the hand of friendship. Not immediately. To say, "Of course, I didn't mean it," would be a timid climb-down, and he was too proud for that, too important in this theatre to humble himself before a lesser member of the company.

He was Stephen Hammond, a public idol, handsome and debonair, whose charm was his greatest asset. Off-stage he had to keep up the pose, and succeeded to such an extent that he could no longer tell when he was posing and when he was not.

The frightening thing about being a public idol was the possibility of losing one's appeal, and during the last twelve months the fear had begun to creep up on him, especially when his dressing-room mirror revealed deepening lines on his face and his hairdresser recommended more and more treatments for thinning hair. To some men these things didn't matter; to Stephen Hammond they mattered a lot. Age was a bogey which he desperately wanted to keep at bay.

★ ★ ★

The note Della had left was characteristic.

'Hail, Sarah Bernhardt! If from your lofty histrionic heights you can toy with the homely spud, you'll find a meat-'n-tattie pie in t'oven — just like mum used to make. Spoke McGee, broke as usual, dropped in to scrounge a bite and wolfed half, so eat the rest before he comes back for more. We are now off to the Rialto on a free pass he got from a newspaper pal — must do something while I wait with bated breath for your return. (May I have your autograph, please, Miss Loren?)'

Susan sat down abruptly, had a good weep, then ate the meat-and-potato pie. She carried it on a tray to the window, then wished she hadn't, for she looked straight across at St. Bede's Hospital and promptly thought of David. She had been doing her best to forget about him and, thanks to Stephen Hammond, had been fairly successful. Stephen had taken her to a little club in Chelsea, comforted her, charmed her, and driven her home in his eye-catching and ear-splitting red sports car. It was a pity that Della wasn't in to see and hear their arrival. Della was a fan of Stephen's and would certainly have forgone a free seat at the Rialto for a glimpse of him.

The lights of St. Bede's were shining into the dusk. Susan turned her back on them and ate the pie with the unquenchable appetite of youth. An hour or two ago she had thought she would never eat again. An hour or two ago she had wondered how she had been able to swallow a mouthful in David Radcliffe's company.

"Cunning," said Stephen. "That's the only word for him, whisking you out of the way like that while his wife wormed her way into your place. I can't understand why Grace gave in to her."

"Because she is a better actress and an experienced one."

It was the only possible answer, and Maxine Culver had been right when she said that an under-study at the Comet was a plum for a newly-fledged drama student, so she ought to count herself lucky instead of wallowing in disappointment.

By the time Della came in Susan had pulled herself together, but now disappointment gave place to anger, especially when she thought of David and the way in which he had drunk to her success.

'*When I thought up the part of Nina, I must have had you in mind.*'

Cunning? He was a heel, two-faced, thoroughly untrustworthy. A married man who dated unmarried girls. She would give him a wide berth in future.

Della sailed in, demanding, "Well? When do you start rehearsing?"

"Later."

"What do you mean — later?"

"That's when under-study rehearsals always begin."

"Under-study? *You*? They must be out of their minds!"

"I'm lucky to get that — a newly-fledged drama student."

"Who said so?"

Susan wanted to answer, "David's wife," and found that she couldn't.

"It doesn't matter," she said. "It's true, anyway."

Della's disappointment was almost as keen as her own. Susan looked at her crestfallen face and said, "Don't look like that. I'm no Sarah Bernhardt, no matter what you may think."

"Well, I *do* think — "

A sharp summons from the front door bell cut into her words.

Outside stood David Radcliffe.

"I counted the windows and worked out which floor you lived on — "

So she couldn't give him a wide berth. Della was looking at him with interest and obviously liking what she saw. Equally obviously, she expected Susan to invite him in — and so did David. She had no choice but to open the door wider for him.

"I couldn't wait to come off duty," he said eagerly. "It's all tied up, of course?"

Susan made polite introductions, and David's glance became puzzled. Her frigid courtesy dampened his eagerness and for a fleeting moment he regretted coming. But he had been so sure of a welcome.

"Oh, yes," said Susan pleasantly, "it's all tied up."

Della looked from one to the other and disappeared into the box of a kitchen, pretending she wasn't around. When they were alone, David said, "What's wrong, Susan?"

"Nothing."

"That isn't true. You're different. You weren't like this at lunch."

"No. At lunch I was happy and trusting and naïve."

The bitterness in her voice alarmed him. He took hold of her shoulders and said, "Come on — tell me. What's gone wrong?"

"For you — nothing."

"For me? I don't know what you mean. The only thing that could go wrong for me would be your failure to get the part."

"Well, I didn't get it. Your wife did."

He didn't move. His hands on her shoulders didn't move. His eyes didn't move.

Susan jerked away.

"I'm to be her under-study. Aren't you pleased?"

"No. I am not pleased."

"Is that all you have to say?" she cried. When he just stood there, making no answer, his mouth set tightly and happiness wiped from his face, she continued wildly, "Well, you *should* be pleased. It all worked according to plan, didn't it? I suppose I ought to congratulate you and I would if only — if only you hadn't said the things you did say — that when you thought up the part of Nina you must have had me in mind — that I'd got the part and Grace Challoner was going to tell me so." To her shame, tears flowed and she brushed them away with the back of her hand, leaving her cheeks smeared. "It wouldn't have been so bad if only you hadn't said all those things!"

"They were true. I meant every word, though what in the name of heaven *you* mean by everything going according to plan I've no idea. Perhaps you'd explain."

There was a note in his voice which frightened her, a steely, angry note, but she threw back at him, "I mean precisely what I say! Stephen knows about it, too.

Cunning, he called it, and I agree!"

David shouted, "If you think for one moment that *I* had anything to do with Maxine getting the part, you're a pretty poor judge of character! Now I'm going to tell you the truth and you can take it or leave it — "

"I don't want to hear — "

He pushed her into a chair.

"You're *going* to hear it. You're going to sit there and listen to every word I say, and when I've finished I'm leaving." She could feel his anger, hot as a flame, and so she sat mutely, doing as she was told.

"First, I had no idea that Maxine was even being auditioned. It was a shock to me when she appeared on the stage. I haven't seen or heard of her for over a year. We were married when I was still a medical student and it lasted fifteen awful months. I couldn't satisfy her in any way and I doubt if any man could. I offered to give her a divorce; she refused, and has gone on refusing. Why, I don't know. She is not religious and, as she frequently reminded me, I'm far from rich. Also, she despised my background.

My people are ordinary, working-class folk from Streatham. My father died just after I qualified and since then I've helped to support my mother. That was another thing Maxine protested about. 'Why can't she go out to work?' she used to say. 'Able-bodied women can always find jobs.' The answer is that I think my mother worked hard enough all her life and it's time she sat back and let others support her, so I and my brothers do just that. I'm not going to give you the unhappy details of my marriage. You're young and you might not understand a lot of it, but sometimes two people can get tied together so tragically that it's hard to believe that God ever joined them together.

"Bit by bit Maxine sapped every ounce of my self-confidence. She ridiculed me. My background, my appearance, my lack of social graces, even my ambitions. I like hospital work; she calls it the squalid side of medicine. Once, when I was doing a casualty shift, she called in to see me. She chose a bad moment — a drug addict was being admitted. She told me later that she couldn't understand why anyone should want to help people like that. I realised then that when she married me she imagined I would become some pinstriped specialist in Harley Street, and *I* realised that I neither will, nor want to, but after that it became an obsession with me to prove myself, to show her, or the world, or maybe myself alone, that I was something more than a boy from the suburbs, and after I had left her — yes, *I* left *her* — I started to write my play.

"Half of it is fact, there's a lot of our marriage in it, and half of it is fiction, or maybe just my dreams. And that is where Nina comes in. And that is why I *know* that Maxine could never play the part and why I wouldn't have lifted a finger to help her to get it, let alone connive in some underhanded little scheme, as you seem to imagine I did. What's more, I'll prove it to you — somehow, *anyhow*, even if I have to break her neck to do it!"

The front door slammed behind him so violently that the room vibrated.

Della put her head tentatively round the kitchen door.

"I tried not to listen," she said, "but I couldn't help hearing. My, but there's a man with a temper! I wouldn't like to get in his way when it was really roused."

9

GRACE telephoned Ethel that evening, feeling a desperate need to talk to someone. She had arrived home to find a message waiting from Philip. The conference had delayed him and an urgent call made it necessary for him to visit his constituency at once. An overnight bag had been packed and sent round to him.

So she was unable to unburden herself to him and turned to Ethel instinctively.

"I've given Maxine the part," she said without preliminary. "As you warned me — I had no choice."

They talked guardedly on the phone.

"I'm going to tell Philip everything," Grace said.

"I think you are wise. He will know what to do, and he loves you deeply."

That was the important thing, the reassuring thing. She could count on his love to protect her — but how could she protect him? If he suffered in any way she would never forgive herself.

Ethel said bitterly, "I wish Maxine would go out of my life and stay out. You read of people like her, but never really believe they exist until you are up against them."

"You had lost touch, hadn't you?"

"Completely. I hadn't seen or heard of her for several years. I have a vague idea she married, but who, I don't know."

"Is she still with him?"

"I doubt it. She told me she had a flat in Bayswater, and I think she regretted telling me even that. It's funny how she makes it her business to know so much about other people, but takes good care to give little away about herself."

But that was typical of her type, thought Grace, feeling sorry for any man who married Maxine.

"I wish I could get hold of the rest of the newspaper cutting. She said she was keeping that back as a safeguard, a kind of insurance so that if the photograph was lost or destroyed she would have the remainder to prove her story. So my tearing it up was a complete waste of time."

"She thinks of everything, doesn't she?" Ethel commented bitterly.

"I shall get rid of her as soon as I can," Grace vowed. "Philip will know how to handle her, and once we have made sure of her silence I can replace her in the cast. I'd like to do that for Susan Howard's sake as well as my own. That girl has talent, and she took her disappointment well to-day."

★ ★ ★

Too well, said Della as the girls prepared for bed that night. "I would have blown my top!" she declared.

"I can't afford to," Susan answered wryly.

She spoke absently, for her thoughts were still occupied with young Doctor Radcliffe. Why should she care if he were married? Why should she mind that he had kept silent about it? They had only met that day and a man didn't have to say to a girl right away, "I think you ought to know that I am married." For all he knew, she might have been, too.

And the fact that he had taken her out

102

to lunch meant nothing. It was a friendly gesture, no more.

"Do you believe him?" Della asked abruptly.

"Believe who?" Susan hedged.

"The angry young man. He handed you a pretty long story about his marriage, didn't he?"

Too long? Too elaborate? Too convincing?

"Do *you* believe him?" Susan asked.

"Oddly enough, yes. The ring of truth penetrated the kitchen door. And he was certainly anxious that you should have it."

It was odd that Della's words should make her happy, but Susan fell asleep feeling strangely comforted.

★ ★ ★

Tom Langley was the first to arrive at the theatre next morning. He was in the dressing-room which served as his office and odd-job room, a luxury not always provided for stage directors, who sometimes had to make do with the prop room in the wings, but as a resident member of the Comet Theatre Company he had acquired this dressing-room at the top of the spiral staircase simply because it was to spare and he could make use of it. Here he did the paper work connected with his job, wrote letters, drew up stage directions for new productions, and put his feet up when he wanted a quiet cigarette.

The door was open when he heard the footsteps on the iron stairs. At first, he didn't heed them, but when they came nearer and he realised that they were not the footsteps of a man, he became curious. The topmost dressing-rooms were reserved for male members of the company, and since the footstep was obviously that of a woman it could only mean that a woman was visiting one of them. This went against the unwritten theatrical law that actresses never visited the actors' dressing-rooms either during or between shows.

What made Tom keep silent, he had no idea. He thought later that the natural thing would have been to make his presence known; instead, he stood there listening, puzzled and surprised. The theatre, apart from himself, was empty, and when members of the company did arrive they would gather on the stage, being summoned one by one into Grace's dressing-room to sign their contracts. After that, rehearsals would begin.

So there was absolutely no reason for a woman to be climbing so far up the spiral staircase, unless she had an appointment with a male member of the cast — one appearing in the current show and therefore already in possession of a dressing-room.

The footsteps stopped. He heard a door open on the floor below and hastily calculated which door it was. The nearest to the iron staircase was Stephen Hammond's, and since the footsteps had not continued along the corridor they had obviously paused there.

But Stephen hadn't arrived. Tom knew that because the usual stack of letters for Stephen had been waiting at the stage-doorkeeper's office. They couldn't be missed, bulging in the pigeon-hole marked H, and overflowing on to the doorkeeper's desk.

Tom took a few steps across the room, then hesitated. Dressing-rooms were always left unlocked so that the cleaners could enter and, since actors never kept anything of more personal value than make-up in the theatre, locks and bolts were unheeded. But at this hour the cleaners had gone. Curiosity stirred, but it wasn't his job to play watch-dog about the place, so what excuse could he offer for snooping, if caught?

No sound came from below. The woman had entered Stephen's dressing-room, presumably with the intention of waiting for him, so the obvious thing for Tom to do was to return to his own room and shut the door. He was about to do so when he detected faint sounds, like the shutting of cupboard doors, or drawers, but couldn't be sure. Then he heard something which definitely disturbed him. A piece of furniture was being shaken impatiently, as if the woman were trying to force a drawer that was locked.

He had no hesitation then, but he had only taken two steps towards the top of the spiral staircase when other footsteps echoed from below. This time a man was coming up and Tom knew his step well.

It was Stephen, and he ran up with the confidence of a man who was familiar with every tread of those perilous stairs.

And still Tom waited. There was no sound from Stephen's dressing-room now.

When Stephen reached his floor he stepped off the iron stairs, crossed to the door of his dressing-room and stood still abruptly.

His voice echoed up the spiral, thrown back from the old stone walls of the building. Even from this height it was possible to hear voices from as far below as the stage.

"What the devil are *you* doing here?" Stephen demanded.

Tom couldn't hear the woman's reply. She was within the room, her voice cut off by the projecting door, but she must have walked across to it, for a moment later the rest of her words came floating up.

" . . . I didn't think I'd have the opportunity to ask you once the company arrived, so I came here to wait for you — and to get you alone. I suppose you'll think it frightfully naïve of me to want your autograph, but I've collected them from every show I've ever been in. I hoped yours would bring me luck at our first rehearsal."

Stephen laughed.

"Do you honestly expect me to believe that? After yesterday?"

"What has yesterday got to do with it?"

"Well, I didn't exactly make you welcome, did I? I made it pretty obvious that I didn't want you in the cast. Mind you, I've nothing against you personally. I simply thought that the Howard girl was more suited to the part. All the same, I wouldn't have been surprised if you hated me for it."

"But I don't hate you! I admire you. I always have and I always will, and I'm thrilled at the thought of appearing in a show with you. Please — can't we be friends? Can't we forget yesterday altogether? Be patient with me, and I'm sure I'll be good in the part. Give me your advice on how to interpret it. I'd appreciate that."

Tom thought wryly, "This is the sort of approach that Stephen is a sucker for.

Talk to him like that, my girl, and he'll eat out of your hand."

He leaned over the iron rail and saw Maxine and Stephen standing just within the door of the dressing-room. Maxine was opening her handbag and taking something out. He couldn't see what it was, but he could see the handbag quite plainly. It was black suède, with an eye catching jade clasp.

"Would you write here?" she was saying. "This is my diary, and if you sign on the date of our first rehearsal I'm sure it will bring me luck."

Stephen signed. He had never been known to refuse. He was psychologically incapable of resisting any form of flattery or compliment, and Maxine's adoration communicated wordlessly and effectively. When he finished writing and handed the diary back he reacted in the usual way, expanding beneath her glance.

"Oh, *thank* you," she breathed.

"And now, be off with you," Stephen said indulgently. "You've no right to be here, you know. Any actress knows that dressing-room visits between the sexes are frowned on by managements. Do you want to stir up gossip in the theatre at the start?"

Maxine laughed.

"I'm going, but I'm not sorry I came. I couldn't bear it yesterday when you said you wanted to wring my neck."

"Correction. I said I'd like to wring your beautiful neck."

"Combining flattery with threat?"

"You know it's a beautiful neck, so you know it isn't flattery."

"But you don't feel like wringing it still, do you?"

"Of course not."

"Now I'm happy again."

She still smiled up at him in that adoring way and Stephen's reaction was inevitable. There were two things this man could not resist — admiration, and a woman. When the two came together he was a pushover.

"Before I go, wish me luck," Maxine pleaded.

Stephen held out his hand.

"I do wish you luck, and now, again, be off with you. I've a batch of mail to deal with."

As Stephen closed his dressing-room

door and Maxine put one foot on the spiral staircase, Tom turned back to his own room, feeling guilty because he had been eaves-dropping. The movement attracted Maxine's attention and her head jerked up. There was surprise in her face and a faint alarm; both were replaced by anger when she saw him. Then she smiled vividly.

"Why, hello there, Tom! I'm so glad we met before rehearsal. I wanted to tell you yesterday how glad I am that you've got on your feet again."

Honeyed words coating a deliberate reminder. So she did know, and hadn't forgotten, and was determined that he should be aware of it.

He turned away, saying nothing, and she laughed softly, then began to descend the stairs. She went more carefully than when she came up. It was easier to climb the stairs on one's toes than to descend that way with stiletto heels that could catch all too easily in the holes of the iron steps.

Tom shut his door and leaned against it. He was shaking and it took him quite a time to control himself. By then,

111

the company had begun to arrive and he knew that Grace would be waiting for him. He had to go downstairs and pretend that nothing had happened to threaten his security.

Maxine Culver hadn't put it into words, but her gentle reminder was every bit as bad as an openly-voiced threat. It told him very plainly that he would be wise to remember that she knew all about his past.

10

"I WANT a word with you, Maxine."

"Why, David, how lovely to see you! I'm glad you arrived before the rest of the company because I've been wanting an opportunity to congratulate you."

"On what?"

"On having your play accepted, of course. I always knew you had it in you to be a playwright."

"You say that *now* — after ridiculing my attempts?"

"Only your earlier ones, darling, and I didn't ridicule. I criticised — constructively. After all, the theatre wasn't your world, as it was mine. You didn't know a thing about stage requirements. I did and, obviously, you've benefited by my help."

He shouted with laughter. "Considering you repeatedly told me that I had no talent and that I should stick to being a third-rate doctor, your change of mind amuses me."

They had met at the foot of the spiral stairs. Maxine strolled towards the stage and David walked beside her.

"I didn't know you were coming to the theatre this morning," she said.

"I wasn't. I came especially to see you."

She glanced at him with slightly raised eyebrows.

"Not Susan Howard? I had the impression yesterday that you were impressed by her, and that was why you carried her off to lunch."

"I was. So impressed that I thought she should have the part. So did everyone else. That is why I can't understand how you got it. How did you pull it off? How did you persuade Grace Challoner?"

She looked at him in slightly pained reproach.

"Won't you even give me the credit for getting the part on my merits? I am an experienced actress, you know."

"Experienced not only as an actress," he said cynically.

Maxine ignored that.

"If you want to know how I persuaded

114

Grace — ask her. Not that she will tell you."

"You make it sound as if you'd blackmailed her into it. Is that your latest talent?"

"I don't know what you mean."

What was the use, he thought despairingly. He wasn't going to get anywhere with Maxine in this mood. He knew her of old. She could be as close as an oyster when it suited her.

"You might at least congratulate me, David."

"On getting your own way by devious means? There's nothing worthy of congratulation in that."

"I see you are as unkind as ever. I should have thought that after all this time you could at least be charitable towards me."

"Charitable! I've paid you a regular monthly allowance and fulfilled all my legal obligations as a husband. Did you ever fulfil yours as a wife? Even when we lived together I knew there were other men in your life, although when it came to proving it you were cleverer than I was."

"Could I help it if men fell in love with me?"

"Past tense? Have they all got wise to you now?"

Her elaborately made-up eyes flickered, the mascaraed lashes veiling her reaction. Her voice became pleading.

"David, you loved me once. For old times' sake, can't you remember that now?"

"Unfortunately, I do remember it. I was mad about you. I idolised you. I suppose that made disillusion even sharper."

"I was young and stupid! Can't you forgive me?" He looked at her suspiciously.

"Please, David — couldn't we start again? These months of separation have taught me a lot. I've grown up, darling." She hurried on, "Oh, I know, you've every cause to say it's about time! Say anything you like, only *try* to forgive me. We could make a new start, I'm sure we could."

"In the same way as before? Dirty rooms and unmade beds, dishes eternally stacked in the sink, overflowing ash-trays, meals out of tins and the tradesmen never paid, not to mention all your seedy hangers-on idling away their unemployed time in *my* home? There are a lot of decent people in the theatre, but you always ganged up with those who weren't, and while I swotted to pass medical exams you played around with the worst possible types, filling the flat with them, record-player going non-stop, supplies of drink from the local off-licence being charged up to *me*. Do you think I want to go back to that sort of life?"

"Do you think *I* want to? I wasn't a model wife and I know it, but I was young — "

"Five years older than me," he reminded her cruelly.

"That didn't prevent you from rushing me off my feet when we met."

"I admit it. I was hopelessly enamoured of you. You were a complete contrast to the world and the life I had known. I had never met a woman like you before — beautiful and sophisticated and experienced. *I* was the one who was young, but I grew up rapidly after

I married you." He gave an impatient sigh. "What's the use of raking over dead ashes?"

"Are they dead?" she said wistfully. "Why do you think I have refused to divorce you?"

"I've often wondered," he murmured bitterly.

"Because in my heart I still love you. I've always hoped we might get together again."

He stared at her in astonishment.

"You surely don't expect me to swallow that? Our life together was hell. You were eternally reminding me of the mistake you made in marrying me. A third-rate doctor you called me again and again and again. Well, it might interest you to know that I'm still plodding the hospital wards and have every intention of continuing to."

"Not when you are a successful playwright, surely?"

"Ah — so that's it! You now see me becoming a second Terence Rattigan, writing plays for you to act in!"

"Why not? We'd be a good team."

"Oh, wonderful," he said cynically. "Have you read this play of mine?"

"Yes. I was handed a script to take home and study last night."

"Then you must have recognised a lot of it. It was our marriage, re-lived. In part, at least. The rest is what I wanted it to be. A dream of the might-have-been. How often do you think I can write plays like that? Only once in a lifetime. This acceptance is no more than a flash-in-the-pan which might even be a flop."

"Not at the Comet. Comet productions are always successful. Darling, you are earmarked for success simply *because* the Comet has accepted you."

"So that is why you want me to come back to you?"

"No!"

"If, and I say *if*, we tried to start again, you would have to accept me as I am — a doctor whose ideas and ambitions don't coincide with your own. You used to hope that I'd become a fashionable specialist in the West End, charging society neurotics spectacular fees, but you very quickly realised there was no hope of that. There are thousands of doctors like me, the steady, plodding types that make medicine their career

119

simply because they are interested in it. They serve in hospitals up and down the country, reaching senior positions in middle-age, never becoming famous or rich or fashionable. That's me, Maxine."

She didn't answer. What was going on in her mind he could only guess at. He saw tight lines of strain behind the mask of her make-up, and guessed that she hadn't found life too easy since their separation, despite the fact that she had bragged that she could get on better without him. Now he wondered what parts she had played, and how many contracts she had managed to land to supplement the allowance he made her.

He felt a faint stirring of pity, the kind of pity he felt for a patient who endeavoured to hide anxiety, but the next minute she exasperated him again by saying, "Other doctors have given up medicine for profitable careers as writers and playwrights. Look at Cronin — "

"I'm not another Cronin. I'm David Radcliffe, on the staff of St. Bede's Hospital and happy to remain there. Take it or leave it."

"And if I take it, you'll come back to me?"

He felt something like panic surge up in him. The thought of living with her again repelled him. It would be life as before, with all its squalor and quarrelling and slowly festering hatred.

"I am still your wife," she reminded him gently.

Clinging, strangling, never letting him go, binding him for ever, standing in the way of freedom and any chance of happiness with someone else. Not that there was anyone else. He was on good terms with the nursing staff at St. Bede's, but never dated anyone. Free, but never free — that was what separation had meant to him. The prospect of living that way for ever depressed him. He wanted a home, a wife, children, the normal things desired by any normal man. If he went back to her, he knew there wasn't the remotest chance of these things coming true. Motherhood had never appealed to Maxine and now he thought with a terrible kind of sadness that in the circumstances it was a good thing his children had remained unborn.

"So you won't agree?" she said, and for a moment the longing in her voice almost had him convinced. Then he saw her eyes and recognised in them a light with which he had become very familiar during their ill-starred partnership — a cold calculation which not even her technical skill as an actress could conceal.

He turned away, saying nothing, and at that moment the heavy door leading from the street opened, and Ethel Fothergill walked through with Grace Challoner.

"Hello, Maxine. So you got the part," her aunt said. "Don't ask me to congratulate you."

"I don't need your congratulations, Auntie dear."

David looked from one to the other. It had been a surprise to him to learn, yesterday when they sat in the stalls, that Ethel was Maxine's aunt, although he vaguely remembered her once mentioning that her mother's sister was on the stage. "A corny old actress in provincial rep. I shall never follow in *her* footsteps!" Now he wondered if Maxine had traded on the relationship after all.

Maxine was herself again — bright and

122

brittle and confident.

"By the way, Ethel, I never introduced you to my husband, did I? Since you know each other now, it is hardly necessary."

Both Ethel and Grace looked surprised, then their glances met. David saw a question flash between them, and was puzzled. Slowly, they looked at him and the question had become speculation.

Maxine laughed. "Don't worry, the pair of you. He doesn't know a thing."

The street door opened again and Susan Howard entered so quietly that no one noticed her. She wore a plain grey dress with a white Puritan collar which made her look even younger than she was. She stood just within the entrance and heard David say, "I don't know what? What are you talking about?"

Ethel answered, "Why didn't you tell us you were Maxine's husband?"

"Why should I?" He looked across and saw Susan and his mouth curved a little bitterly. "If you want to know the truth about our marriage, ask Susan. She knows it but, like her, I don't suppose you'll believe it."

Grace said in a tired voice, "It is no concern of ours, anyway. Is everyone here? I'd like to get started as soon as possible."

"Started on what?" David said. "If you mean on rehearsals for my play, I'm sorry, but I'm withdrawing it." When the others could do nothing but stare he continued defensively, "Why shouldn't I? It is my play, my property. If I decide not to let it be produced — "

"You can't do that," Grace told him. "Comet bought the rights. You signed a contract."

But suddenly her mind was racing, wondering whether postponed production would keep Maxine at bay for a while; then she decided that it was just as likely to provoke the girl into immediate action.

It was Philip she needed, and she needed him badly. She wished from the bottom of her heart that he would come home.

David walked out of the theatre, not glancing at Susan. He was very much aware that the girl was free, and he was not. He even felt less free to-day than he did yesterday, for Maxine had come back into his life, reminding him of their relationship, wanting to restore it to its old footing, begging to be his wife again in more than name.

He walked back to the hospital, deep in thought. His upbringing had been conventional, based on the teaching that man and wife remained man and wife until death did them part, but that had been easy enough for his parents, who had loved each other and been happy together, his father the bread-winner and his mother content to be housewife. Home life had been real home life in their suburban house. Meals were properly cooked and the house was properly cleaned and they owed no man a penny. His mother paid cash across the counter for provisions, and what they couldn't afford they did without.

To Joseph and Hilda Radcliffe their children were their life, worth making sacrifices for, worth struggling for. It had been beyond their comprehension that people could live any other way, or that marriage could survive in any other fashion. It was inevitable that David had absorbed their teaching, so that even now he felt a sense of responsibility towards the woman he had made his wife. If he took legal advice on the situation he knew what it would be — try for a reconciliation. But how could there be a reconciliation or any hope of happiness with a woman he no longer loved and who, he was sure, had never really loved him?

And all the time he kept remembering Susan, and the way in which he had been attracted to her during their celebration lunch. The girl was young, with a good career ahead of her. She was free to fall in love and marry, but he was not. Their attraction had to stop before it went any further.

And the best way of stopping it would be to return to his wife, to try to make a success of his marriage again, because there was certainly no hope of death parting them and until it did they were tied together.

11

REHEARSALS started punctually. Susan watched from an unobtrusive seat in the stalls, with the usual self-effacement of under-studies. She wished that David had remained, or that he had at least given her the chance to assure him that she did believe what he said. She was confident in her own mind that he had had nothing to do with Maxine getting the part. He was too blunt, too forthright, too honest. His punches came straight from the shoulder; he would never stab in the back.

She deliberately thrust down the disappointment she felt because he had virtually ignored her this morning. She had to rid her mind of all thought of him, because Maxine was still his wife and so long as she remained his wife there was always a chance that they would get together again. And that, of course, was as it should be. Her own parents had stuck together through thick and thin, and this, she had been brought up to believe, was marriage. Perhaps, even yet, David and Maxine would make a success of it.

Once rehearsals began Susan became absorbed. The highly-skilled first reading impressed her, being very different from the students' performances she was accustomed to. Here there was no uncertain groping, no self-consciousness, no tendency to over-act, and everything proceeded in a smooth, relaxed, and easy-going way.

It wasn't until the second run-through, the next day, that she began to see the other side of the picture, when the players were expected to be more familiar with their lines and, by the third day, almost word-perfect for the whole of the first act. Then the high standard required of professional actors was really brought home to her. Any trace of leniency had gone.

Grace had handed over the production of *Wings of Morning* to Stephen, and from him Tom Langley took his stage directions. At first, Stephen proceeded gently, using his charm on the cast, and all went well so long as he was concerned only with producing, but difficulties arose when he was involved as an actor. He no longer seemed capable of being an actor-producer, and it became obvious to Grace that he would have to concentrate solely on acting in the future. He was becoming more and more temperamental, more unpredictable, with an increasing tendency to resort to rage. She decided that once this production was launched she would engage an outside producer for the next show, whether Stephen liked the idea or not.

But Stephen's anger could evaporate quickly, giving way to good humour. After a ten-minute break he would return full of affability and zest. He swung like a pendulum between depression and elation, which might indicate the artistic temperament, Susan thought, but as a thing to work with was certainly trying. She wasn't surprised when members of the cast became either discouraged or infuriated, and sometimes wondered how any co-operation could be achieved under such erratic leadership. Tears flowed, tempers flared, words became heated, only to subside into reconciliation scenes and pleas for forgiveness.

Theatrical people were certainly emotional, she thought, and wondered how David, from the practical world of medicine, would react were he here. Tension seemed to be gathering in the theatre, although what caused it she could not decide.

David stubbornly kept away from rehearsals, despite Grace's invitation to attend. "I'm busy at the hospital," he said, which was true enough, but Maxine guessed, and rightly, that he stayed away because he wanted to avoid her. The thought was neither pleasing, nor flattering, and her failure to appeal to him the other day made her want him all the more.

She had been surprised when his play had been accepted. "By David Radcliffe, an unknown doctor," she had seen in a theatrical magazine one day, when reading about the Comet's next production, and she realised at once that despite her lack of faith in his ability as a playwright her husband had actually pulled it off.

From that moment she began to think

about him quite a lot. All along her instinct for self-preservation had urged her not to cut herself off from him completely. A husband was always a lifeline in a woman's life, and it gave Maxine a sense of security to know that she had a man to fall back on, a man who had taken the initial step in the break-up of their marriage, which gave her the legal right to be supported by him still. It would have been a different story had she been the one to walk out.

It hadn't broken her heart when he went, and she had made no attempt to get him back, but now that life had ceased to be either kind or generous to her and men didn't respond so easily or so frequently, she was glad that she had had the foresight to refuse to divorce him. Economically, if for no other reason, he might be glad to return to her; a man might well consider that he should at least have something for his money, even if it was only a rather second-rate housekeeper. She was honest enough to admit that running a home was not her line, but now she began to think that it might be a good idea to make it so.

Once past the age of thirty a woman saw forty beckoning ahead, and had second thoughts about a lot of things. In particular, her future.

It never occurred to Maxine that she was either ruthless or unscrupulous. She was simply following a code of her father's — a scoundrel if ever there was one, but a scoundrel she had admired far more than she had admired her gentle, ineffectual mother.

"Make up your mind what you want, my girl, and go right out after it. Get it, it doesn't matter how, and let no one stop you. That's the way to get to the top."

Sometimes she remembered that it hadn't got him to the top, but it still seemed a sound doctrine to her and, so far, had always paid off because she was actually more astute than her father had been. In his time he had made his packet, but lost it all in the end, the trouble with him being that he wasn't shrewd in his judgment of people, as she was. She knew how to use them, how to get things out of them, how to manipulate and control them.

People were puppets, she thought

132

contemptuously. All one had to do to make them dance was to pull the strings, as she was pulling them now, jerking poor old Auntie Ethel and the beautiful, but foolish, Grace Challoner. These two would do to go on with, but it was good to know that she had something on poor old Tom Langley as well. (*That* might come in useful, some time!) Add to these a close relationship with the author of the play, and her foot could be well inside the door.

With luck, she would penetrate even further. She hadn't been a doctor's wife for nothing and Stephen Hammond revealed symptoms which the lay person would only be puzzled by, but once before she had seen a horrible demonstration of these symptoms in an advanced stage. Stephen hadn't reached it yet, although if he continued on his crazy way he certainly would. Meanwhile, she wondered if he was aware that she not only knew his secret but had evidence of it. Looking back to their meeting in his dressing-room the other morning, she felt that only a fool would have failed to guess that she was responsible for that forced lock and empty drawer. It must have stared him in the face after she left. It amused her to think that he was now reaching a state of frenzy because of it.

This, no doubt, was why he was giving her a tough time at rehearsal, and the longer she allowed him to, the worse he would get, and the stronger her power. She would get her own back — in time.

It almost seemed as if he were determined to make her fail in the part.

"Can't you feel this girl's suffering?" he demanded at rehearsal one morning. "Can't you *feel* it, for heaven's sake? Let's take the scene again . . ."

So they took it again and yet again, while the rest of the cast looked on. She portrayed Nina's suffering with all the technical skill at her command. She couldn't see anything wrong with that, but he could. Pounding on the rail of the orchestra pit with angry fists, he shouted at her from the stalls, "*Feel* it, can't you? Don't just go through the motions! Feel it from your heart — *here*! You'll never move an audience to tears if you can't

134

shed them yourself!"

All these tedious histrionics, she thought wearily. How unnecessary they were! A drop or two of glycerine on the cheeks, the film stars' trick, and who could tell the difference? And that way one's mascara didn't run.

She was wise enough never to blaze back at him, but resentment began to smoulder inside her. Wait, just *wait*, she vowed silently. I'll pay you back for every jibe and sneer, for every bullying word, for every smothered titter from the wings, for every humiliating moment when, in front of the whole company, you've ridiculed me as an actress, and if you're trying to make me throw up the part, you will never, never, *never* succeed. It is mine, and I'm hanging on to it. I need the money, as well as the prestige of working in London again, and no screaming neurotic is going to cheat me out of that. If anyone throws in the sponge, my handsome, ageing idol of stage and screen, it will be you.

★ ★ ★

Stephen wondered for the hundredth time just why Grace had insisted on engaging Maxine. The girl was slick, good-looking, and full of technical tricks; she knew how to walk, how to move, how to pitch her voice, but she had no emotions. Producing her in a part was like playing on a piano that had all the keys, but no depths of tone — all right for banging out a tune on, but not for playing a symphony.

Either she goes, or I will, he thought despairingly. It will come to that in the end.

He felt exhausted, and depression was clamping down on him like a heavy hand. Once upon a time a quick drink would have revived him, but not any more. Alcohol only fuddled him now; he needed something else to clear his brain and revive his spirits, to give him back the boundless vitality which had once been his, to make him feel young and confident again. To make him feel like a king.

After four days of rehearsals he was already beginning to flag. He told himself that it was entirely due to Grace's

136

insistence on mis-casting the part of Nina. If she had given him better material to work with, the right girl for the part, none of these difficulties would have arisen and the sick apprehension he had endured ever since Maxine's unexpected visit to his dressing-room would never have taken hold of him.

He had never heard of Maxine Culver before she turned up for the audition that day; never even knew that Ethel Fothergill had a niece. Why Grace had to engage the girl just for that reason (and what other could there be?) he couldn't imagine. It had always been a policy of the Comet Theatre Company — which meant Grace's policy, since the company was really hers — never to let influence play a part in things, but what else was she doing now?

Then he remembered that Maxine was David Radcliffe's wife and that he, Stephen, had accused them both of conspiring so that she should get the part. Characteristically, his accusations had been impetuous and only half meant and, characteristically, they had been quickly forgotten, but now that he searched around in his mind for other reasons for blaming Grace, this was added to them.

He decided to have a show-down with her at the earliest opportunity. He would accuse her of allowing both Maxine's aunt *and* her husband to bring pressure to bear. He would issue an ultimatum. "Either she goes, or I do!" It sounded final and very dramatic, but now he remembered that he had said that once before and Grace had merely told him to grow up.

His despair deepened. He ran his hands through his over-long hair — not only was it fashionable now, but he believed it made him look younger — and realised that they were shaking again. They had begun to do that a lot lately, without warning. Nerves were the cause, overwork; tension; the stress of a new production that wasn't going well; frustration because he couldn't have his own way; irritation because, for the first time in their partnership, Grace had completely overruled him.

He took her action as a snub, and resented it.

Now he looked down at his trembling hands, as if they belonged to some pathetic stranger. He had always been proud of his hands and knew them to be one of his most expressive features. He used them a lot when acting, aware that the audience admired them — as they admired everything about him. His looks, his voice, his carriage, his talent, his charm. Oh, dear God, he thought, if I lose all these, what shall I do? If my hands begin to betray me, what next?

A man couldn't keep his looks for ever, or his charm; even a voice could become querulous and weak. The day would come when he would have to rely on his acting ability alone, playing character parts, senile old men or bluff old colonels or quavering grandfathers. The thought made him shudder. When the day came that his fan mail no longer overflowed on to the stage-doorkeeper's desk, it would be his death knell.

The swiftness with which he sank into depression these days was frightening, and it settled on him now like a dark and smothering cloud. He tried to pull himself out of it, and failed. He became aware that one of the actors on the stage was saying something; not the lines in the play, but something to *him*, Stephen Hammond, the producer down in the stalls.

He jerked to attention and the man, a lesser actor in the cast, repeated, "Don't you think it would be better if I moved up right at this point? Miss Culver masks me if I stand here."

"Good grief!" Stephen shouted. "Does it *matter* if the audience can't see you for a couple of minutes? Is that all you think about — your own position, your own share of the spotlight?"

The actor looked aggrieved, as well he might. If anyone ever protested about being 'covered' by another player, it was Stephen himself. Besides, everyone knew that that sort of thing was bad production. Every actor should be seen by the audience at every moment of the play; no one should mask another, or obstruct the delivery of their words.

"Sorry," the man muttered. "I thought these things were important, that's all."

Grace said, "He's right, Stephen, and you don't have to bark at him like that.

140

What's the matter with you?"

"What's the matter with all of us?" he demanded furiously, and thrust his shaking hands into his pockets. "I need a drink. Let's break for half an hour."

"No. There'll be no drinking during rehearsals. We've never allowed that, and you know it. If you feel under the weather, go home and rest. I'll take over."

He was aware that there was concern in her voice as well as annoyance; sympathy as well as irritation. He turned to her and said in a lowered voice, "Grace, will you *please* get rid of that Culver girl? There's something about her — I don't know what it is, but she gets under my skin. It's as if she's watching me all the time. Spying on me. I can't stand it — or her."

Grace looked at him in surprise.

"My dear Stephen, you're imagining things. Rehearsals have only been going four days. Give her a chance to improve."

"She'll never improve because she has nothing to improve *with*. No feeling, no depth, no real emotion. There's nothing there for me to bring out of her, don't

141

you understand? Reciting lines in a crisp professional fashion isn't enough. Not for a part like this."

Grace didn't answer. He saw that her mouth was set tightly and her face looked drawn.

"I can't get rid of her," she said finally. "Not yet."

"*Why*, in heaven's name?"

Again, no answer.

Four days, she was thinking unhappily. Four whole days, and still Philip hadn't come home. Four days in the Midlands, touring his constituency.

Every night he had telephoned her, saying he hoped to be back next day, and every day something cropped up to delay him. Four times she had begged him to come back, and four times she had been unable to tell him how desperately she needed him. It was impossible to say over the telephone that she was in terrible trouble, that she was frightened, that someone could do what they liked with her, threaten, intimidate, and dictate to her, and that it could mean suffering for both of them. Telephones had ears. She could only tell her husband the truth in the privacy of their home, with the door closed upon the world.

She was calculating how many miles away the Midlands were and how long it would take her to reach him if she got into her car the minute rehearsals ended to-day and drove non-stop, when someone sat down beside her and put a hand over hers, and she realised with a wild and incredulous sense of relief that it was Philip himself.

"Surprised?" he whispered with his characteristic smile. "I caught an early-morning train and came straight here."

Her fingers twined about his with such trembling urgency that he looked at her in concern.

She couldn't speak. He held her hand more tightly, studying her in the gloomy light of the theatre, seeing shadows beneath her eyes and tension about her lovely mouth, and knew at once that something was radically wrong.

"I'm taking you home," he said decisively, and when Stephen turned with an impatient demand for silence Philip looked at him with the firm glance that never failed to quell opponents.

It had its effect now. Stephen slumped down in his seat and thought, To hell with everything! — how can I conduct a rehearsal when the leading lady walks out? But he hadn't the nerve to assert his authority as producer. Besides, he always felt out of his depth with Philip Dunster and had no wish to cross him. Anyone who tried would be very effectively dealt with. Stephen wished he had Philip's strength of character. If he had, he would sack Maxine Culver without batting an eyelid, or demand that Grace should do so — *and* make her.

But Stephen hadn't Philip's strength of character, and well he knew it. The only courage he could summon was artificially stimulated, and he badly needed that stimulation now. He called a halt to the rehearsal, although it needed half an hour to go before the appointed time. He saw Maxine saunter off-stage with a contemptuous little smile in his direction and felt, once again, that she knew precisely how he was feeling, and why. Not for the first time, he was frightened by her. Not for the first time, he wished he could get rid of her.

144

Walking through the heavy iron pass door to the stage, Philip and Grace came face to face with a young woman just making her exit. She was dark and striking and, like many a man before him, Philip noticed her at once. What particularly caught his eye was the glance she had for him — bold, smiling, speculative, the kind of glance he had received from many a woman before. Usually he felt either amusement or irritation, for with Grace as his wife he had no need for women of that kind and always brushed them aside, but on this occasion it was not possible. The girl paused deliberately, so that Grace was forced to introduce them.

"This is the actress who is to play Nina," she said, which was an odd sort of introduction, omitting the girl's name, but Philip remembered a conversation in their bedroom the previous Sunday night and said, "The girl who won the bronze medal? The one Stephen spotted at RADA?"

His tone was surprised, because he had imagined someone young and possibly diffident, not a slightly older woman

145

bursting with self-confidence that amounted almost to aggression.

"No," said Grace, "this is Ethel's niece, Maxine Culver."

Grace walked on, leaving Philip to acknowledge Maxine only briefly. There was something about the girl's smile that disturbed him. It was a knowing, amused little smile, full of a strange significance, as if she knew why Grace didn't linger and enjoyed hugging the knowledge to herself. Philip immediately mistrusted her, and as he followed his wife outside he said, "I thought you didn't want Maxine Culver in the company."

"I don't!" Grace declared forcefully. "More than anything in the world I want to get rid of her."

"Then do so, darling."

"I can't." Her voice was taut and strained, totally unlike her usual self.

Philip was scanning the street for a cruising taxi and pretended not to notice his wife's tension.

"Why not?" he asked casually.

"I'll tell you as soon as we get home," Grace said. "I'll tell you everything then."

12

SOMETIMES a playwright could be an irritation in a theatre, interfering with the producer, arguing with members of the cast, throwing his weight around and generally making a nuisance of himself, but no one could accuse David Radcliffe of that. The first time he attended a rehearsal was that afternoon, and his arrival was unobtrusive.

Like Philip Dunster, he entered by the front of the house, slipping quietly into a seat in the stalls and hoping that no one would notice him, especially Maxine. Since their last meeting he had done a lot of thinking, and had come to a definite decision. He would tell her that decision in his own good time, but, knowing Maxine, was aware that she would demand it in hers. So for the time being he wished to remain unobserved, clinging to a temporary peace.

As he sat down, lowering the seat carefully to avoid making any noise, he decided that it might have been better to stay away from the theatre altogether, but if he had done so he had no doubt that Maxine would have gone out of her way to contact him, arriving unheralded at the hospital and attracting comment and attention. His marriage was known to a few of the medical staff who knew him in his student days, and one or two might well remember his wife, for she had never had any compunction about dropping in at the hospital during his duty hours, unethical as this was for doctors' wives.

Besides, the urge to see how his play was progressing had finally overcome him, so here he was, slipping into the stalls at three o'clock in the afternoon, freed from hospital duty until nine in the evening, when he took over on Casualty again.

But there was another reason for coming to the theatre this morning. He wanted to see Susan again, despite his determination to reject her. Not necessarily to talk to her, he insisted, but just to look at her. There was no harm in that.

He looked around now, and saw her sitting a little way off, her eyes on the stage, absorbed in the rehearsal. In the gloomy auditorium her eyes looked over-large, her face a pale oval.

The scene being rehearsed was a love scene between the two principals, and was being acted with Grace and Stephen's customary skill.

Here and there in the auditorium, players not involved in the action, or not waiting for cues in the wings, sat singly or in groups. Susan looked a little solitary, a little out of things, the unimportant under-study whose job it was to remain in the background.

David was tempted to join her, then decided that he might not be welcome. Last time they met he had lost his temper and slammed his way out of her flat — not a well-mannered performance, and he didn't want to risk a snub in return, or to receive nothing but a chill little smile.

Then he saw one of the minor actors walk over to join her, and knew he had done the right thing in leaving her alone. She should be free to enjoy herself with people as unattached as herself.

Someone said his name quietly from the row behind. He recognised the voice at once. Maxine had slipped into the seat behind his own and was letting him know that she was there — close beside him and resolutely remaining so.

He acknowledged her briefly, merely turning to glance over his shoulder then back again to the stage. This was to remind her that the principals were rehearsing and theatrical etiquette therefore demanded complete silence, but all Maxine did was to laugh softly.

"Stephen is fluffing his lines," she whispered. "Haven't you noticed?"

"It is early days," David whispered back.

"So it is for all of us, but he pounces like a tiger if anyone else does it, even at this stage. What's sauce for the goose is sauce for the gander, don't you agree?"

When David made no answer she continued, "The same goes for punctuality. Dear Grace is a stickler for it, and yet she arrived back this afternoon nearly an hour and a half late. Stephen was pacing up and down like a restless horse raring to

150

go, and hit the ceiling when at last she did appear."

Maxine paused, then added in a loud stage whisper, "*It's a pity about Stephen, don't you think?*"

David suppressed a start. So Maxine knew — or had guessed. He felt a deep surge of pity for Stephen Hammond and pretended not to hear what Maxine had said.

Someone ought to help the man, David thought compassionately, and wondered how he could possibly suggest it, or if Stephen would only thrust the offer aside, furious at the suggestion.

"So you're not talking?" Maxine went on with gentle raillery. "Never mind — I can wait."

"For what?"

"You know perfectly well 'for what'," she retorted, impatience lending a sharpness to her voice so that he made a warning gesture for silence and someone in the auditorium uttered a sharp, "*Ssh!*"

David saw Stephen Hammond shoot a glance across the footlights. This made the man miss his cue and beads of sweat

151

broke out on his forehead. There was silence in the theatre while he pulled himself together, then he picked up the scene again and the rehearsing continued.

Still leaning on the back of David's seat, Maxine said close to his ear, "I know why dear Grace was late. Her doting husband turned up this morning and whisked her away before rehearsal was over. She was looking a wreck, too — hardly a sight to gladden a returning husband's eye. He took her home at once, and my guess is that he ordered her to bed for a while — or took her there. Would that have been your prescription, too, dear doctor?"

He remembered that Maxine's gentle teasing had always held a malicious undercurrent, like poison in a perfume. Apparently she hadn't changed.

Stephen fluffed another line and the assistant stage manager, sitting in the prompt corner, put him right at once. Stephen rounded on him.

"Give me a chance to remember the words!" he shouted. "Don't hurl them at me the instant I pause to take breath!"

"Happy little company, aren't we?"

sniggered Maxine. David made no answer, but the antagonism in the theatre did not escape him.

It was obvious that Stephen was ashamed of his outburst, and was about to apologise when Maxine made things worse by tittering audibly.

"Did you have to do that?" David demanded under his breath.

"Yes, darling, I did, and if you hadn't kept away from rehearsals you would know why. It was to pay back our ageing lover for every off-stage snigger I have had to endure through him. Why shouldn't he have a dose of his own medicine?"

"Why not, indeed, if you want to be thrown out of the cast?"

"He can't throw me out. Only the beautiful Grace can do that, and she wouldn't dare."

David was even more conscious of tension in the theatre and wondered how long it had been there, whether it had been building up during the last four days, or whether the seed had been planted even before rehearsals began. Maxine's hint about Grace not daring to get rid of her seemed to hold an ugly significance.

"What are you up to?" he asked abruptly.

"Why should I be up to anything?" Maxine murmured in an injured tone.

"Because it would be out of character if you weren't. I know you from the past."

"And what of the future? Have you made up your mind about that? Are we going to make a new start?"

"It wouldn't be a new start. It would be a repetition of the old one, so the answer is no. Not now or ever."

"That's a pity, because not now or ever will I free you. Just try to get rid of me — *if* you can."

It was then that Maxine realised that Tom Langley was beside her. He had come through the pass door from backstage and down into the auditorium, making his way along the row to her so quietly that she had been quite unaware of him. Now she wondered how long he had been there and how much he had heard. Not that it really mattered, she thought with a mental shrug. She

154

had said nothing that the whole world couldn't be permitted to hear.

"Do you want me?" she asked a little sharply.

"*I* don't, but someone on the telephone does."

She didn't like his tone, but then she didn't like him, either. She regarded him as a stupid old man, always fussing over Grace Challoner like a silly old grandfather. She could guess why. Grace had salvaged him from the wreck of his life and now he would do anything for her. Maxine had been aware, ever since that moment in Grace's dressing-room, that Tom's seemingly guileless old eyes missed nothing. That was why she had reminded him, as he looked down the spiral staircase at her on Tuesday morning, that she remembered all about that unfortunate episode in an otherwise blameless past.

"Who is it?" she asked.

"He didn't give his name."

Not that it had been necessary. Tom had recognised the man's voice at once, and now he watched Maxine's departure in a speculative sort of way, wondering why Philip Dunster, of all people, should be telephoning her.

That was Friday, and as rehearsals were never held on Saturdays until the opening of a new play drew near, Tom Langley called the first run-through for under-studies instead.

"Eleven o'clock sharp," he announced, but Susan arrived half an hour early, being dropped at the theatre by Della and the attentive Spike McGee, who, this time, had scrounged a car from a pal in the motor trade. They were off to Sonning for the day.

The stage-doorkeeper was absent and Susan made her way down to a deserted stage. The safety curtain had not yet been taken up, so the place was almost pitch dark. She shivered a little. Now she could well believe that old theatres were haunted, for although the place was empty she had the strangest feeling that she was not alone, and the even stranger feeling that although she didn't actually hear it, a door somewhere had shut quickly and silently.

Across the stage, in the shadowy wings, she could see a dark mass which was the spiral staircase curling upwards, leading to deserted dressing-rooms and the distant galleries which were known in the theatre as the flies. The whole place was eerie and Susan decided to go for a walk rather than wait around.

As she turned towards the exit she again had the feeling that she was not alone. She paused, holding her breath but hearing nothing except the vague back-stage noises to which all ancient theatres were prone — the rustle of mice in the property room, the faint whistle of air through the floor-boards from the vast area beneath the stage, the creak of scenery stirred by an off-stage draught. There was no real cause for alarm, but she hurried through the exit door, running up the stone steps to street level, her heels clacking like castanets.

She walked briskly, feeling tensed-up and nervous about the rehearsal ahead, so she turned into a coffee bar. It was deserted, and she was served promptly. The coffee resembled coffee in nothing but price, but she drank it gratefully, then walked briskly back to the theatre.

Glancing at her watch she saw to her

surprise that she had been no more than fifteen minutes. It was now a quarter to eleven and others would be arriving.

The first person she saw, turning into the stage door ahead of her, was David. She put out her hand to catch the door as he let it fall behind him and he turned, saw her, and stood still. For a moment they looked at each other, then he said, "I suppose I ought to apologise for my behaviour the other night, losing my temper and slamming out of your flat like that."

"And do you apologise?" she answered with a smile.

At once the tension between them snapped. He held out his hand and she put hers into it.

"Am I forgiven?" he asked.

"There's nothing to forgive. You had every right to blow your top." As they walked down the steps towards the stage she added, "I didn't expect the author to attend under-study rehearsals."

"I came to watch you," he confessed.

It was a simple admission and made her ridiculously happy.

In her absence someone else had

arrived. The stage was still in darkness, but light spilled through the open door of Grace Challoner's dressing-room, opening directly off the wings.

Susan was surprised. She said, "I thought only the stage director attended under-study rehearsals."

"I thought so, too." Then David said sharply, "Wait!"

Susan looked at him, puzzled and surprised, then saw that his glance was focused on the other side of the stage. The spiral staircase could be seen more clearly in the light from the star dressing-room, its top half still in shadow, but the lower half revealed.

So, too, was the thing that lay beneath it.

Time stopped in a frozen minute of suspended silence, then David hurried across the stage.

From beneath the first spiral, a pair of ankles protruded. They belonged to a woman and were clad in sheer nylon and stiletto-heeled shoes.

"Keep away, Susan. Stay where you are."

But she was beside him as he stooped

over Maxine's inert figure.

It was very plain that she had pitched down the central well of the stairs. One spiked heel had snapped off like a twig, presumably caught in one of the small holes of the iron steps. Her stockings were ripped and blood was slowly oozing through. All this Susan observed through a haze of shock.

David's observation was thorough and professional. He lifted his wife's head carefully, examining the back of the skull and neck, then laid it down gently. He felt her pulse, but when he had done so he didn't release her wrist. For a long and careful moment he scrutinised her fingers. Despite his calm, professional attention Susan knew that he was deeply shocked.

There was a sound from Grace Challoner's dressing-room, and simultaneously they turned towards it. Philip Dunster stood in the open doorway, silhouetted against the light which shone from an outside window. He held something in one hand, but it wasn't until later that Susan noticed what it was.

He said, "I've been trying to telephone for a doctor, but the stage-doorkeeper isn't on the switchboard and I can't get an outside line. We'll have to do it from his office. Do either of you know how to operate that thing?"

His voice was matter-of-fact, as if finding a body at the foot of a spiral staircase was nothing really out of the ordinary.

David said, "I am a doctor, so there's no need to call one. I take it you are Miss Challoner's husband?"

"And you?"

"David Radcliffe."

"Author of the new play? I'm sorry we have to meet for the first time in such circumstances."

David was already on his way to the stage-doorkeeper's office. He said over his shoulder, "I'll arrange for her to be admitted to St. Bede's at once."

"Then she isn't dead?" Philip Dunster asked quickly.

"By a miracle, no."

David had opened the exit door. Now he looked back briefly and said, "Don't touch her, whatever you do."

The door closed behind him. Susan could hear his footsteps mounting the stone stairs two at a time. She was alone with Philip Dunster and Maxine's crumpled body.

And it was then that she noticed the thing he held. It was a black suède handbag, with an eye-catching jade clasp.

His glance followed Susan's, and as if in explanation he said, "It was lucky that I came to collect my wife's handbag. She left it behind in her dressing-room last night. If I hadn't dropped in for it in passing, this poor girl might have lain here for a long time without being discovered."

"No," said Susan, her voice jerking painfully. The sight of Maxine lying broken on the floor, her face dead white against a widening pool of blood, had almost unnerved her. "There was an under-study call," she managed to say. "She would have been found then."

If speaking was an effort, coherent thought was worse, but her brain was racing, ticking backwards as she scoured her memory for some recollection as to where she had seen that handbag before.

It was the kind one noticed; elegant and distinctive, and somehow it seemed important to recall something about it.

Suddenly, she did so. She had seen Maxine carrying it several times. It belonged to her, not to Grace Challoner.

13

THE door from the street opened and Tom Langley walked in. He wore his usual wide-brimmed hat with his coat slung cloakwise over his shoulders, looking for all the world like an actor from Edwardian times. A Thermos flask tucked under his arm struck an incongruous note.

He placed it on the stage manager's small table in the prompt corner, laid his coat carefully over the back of a chair, and poured himself some coffee.

"Bless the Trattoria," he said, "they fill this flask for me every morning as I arrive at the theatre. My landlady is excellent, but she cannot make coffee the Italian way. Would you like a cup, Susan?"

"I've had some," she said, and he looked at her sharply from beneath bushy eyebrows.

"Anything the matter, my dear? Not nervous about the rehearsal, are you?

You needn't be. The first understudy run-through is never very demanding. Why, good morning, Mr. Dunster — I didn't see you there. Is Grace here? I wasn't expecting her this morning." He looked surprised, but he went on, "I saw young Doctor Radcliffe fiddling with the telephone switchboard when I came in — I wasn't expecting him, either. Anyway, I didn't offer to help because I've never been able to master that damned thing. He seemed in a hurry, too."

Philip Dunster said, "He is calling an ambulance."

"An *amb* — ?" Tom's glance followed Philip's and he broke off abruptly. "Good God! How did that happen?"

"Obviously, she fell down the spiral staircase."

David returned, saying that an ambulance was coming.

"And the doorkeeper has arrived. Apparently he doesn't come on duty until eleven on Saturdays. I told him to send everyone away. I hope that's all right with you, Langley?"

Tom was staring in horror at Maxine

and replied absently, "Of course, of course . . . "

It was plain that no one would be in the mood for rehearsing now.

Philip Dunster said, "I take it I won't be needed, now everything is under control."

David didn't answer. He was kneeling beside Maxine again, studying the side of her head, but not touching it. Blood was trickling from the back of the skull. He picked up one hand and then the other, examining the fingers closely.

"Just tell me how you found her, will you? I assume she was in this position. You didn't move her, or touch her?"

Philip Dunster said, "Definitely not. I couldn't find a light switch when I arrived, so I groped my way across the stage to my wife's dressing-room. As I came out, the light behind me shone straight on to — on to this girl's body. I went back to telephone at once, then you came. Is she badly injured?"

"A thorough examination can't be carried out until we get her to hospital, but I'd guess that her injuries are extensive and her skull is fractured.

It might be even worse. Brain injuries can be deep, and hard to detect at a glance."

He was still the carefully controlled doctor, but underneath, Susan could tell that he was shaken. This woman was his wife and her injuries might be fatal. Susan stood there helplessly, wishing she could do something, say something, but there was nothing to do but wait for the ambulance to arrive.

Philip said, "Well, if there's really nothing I can do . . . " and turned to the door. As he walked away he said, "This will be a terrible shock for Grace. We'll telephone the hospital later for news."

Tom Langley suggested that someone should let Ethel Fothergill know. "After all, she is Maxine's aunt."

"I'll ask Grace to do it. I think it would be better coming from her, than from a man."

David didn't seem to hear any of this. He had taken off his jacket and placed it over his wife's twisted legs, and then, from outside, the sound of an ambulance bell rang louder and nearer, and soon Maxine was being lifted carefully on to a stretcher and covered with a hospital grey rug. And then she was gone, rushing through the crowded London streets with the ambulance bell ringing and the blue light flashing and the traffic falling away on either side as she was rushed through.

Her husband sat beside the stretcher. His face was grim and set and an ambulance attendant looked at the accompanying nurse, and away again. When a doctor looked like that, they both knew what it meant.

★ ★ ★

Back at the theatre, Tom Langley stared at the spot where Maxine had fallen. He didn't go near it; just stood where he was by the prompt corner, staring at the dark stain on the floor as if he were wondering whose job it was to clear it up. He poured another cup of coffee with a slightly shaking hand and held it out to Susan.

"You'd better have this, my dear, it will do you good."

She drank it automatically, and it did do her good. It was hot, black, and strong, and she felt it coursing through her in a stimulating tide.

Philip Dunster said sympathetically, "That was a horrible shock for you. You'll feel better when you get outside. Can I run you home?"

"No — no, thank you. I'd like to walk."

She needed exercise and movement; fresh air and light. More than anything, she needed to be alone.

Philip nodded understandingly, said good-bye, and turned away finally.

But Susan called after him, "Shall I take that, Mr. Dunster?"

He paused and looked back.

"Take what?"

"Miss Culver's handbag. I see you picked it up."

His hesitation was imperceptible before he answered in surprise, "Is this hers?"

"Oh, yes. I recognise it. She carried it always. I live opposite the hospital, so I'll drop it in for her."

Tom Langley said wryly, "I doubt if she's going to be interested in her handbag for a long time."

"All the same, I'd better take it along. It does belong to her."

She held out her hand for the bag and Philip handed it over. "My mistake. I thought it was my wife's. I'd better look around again for hers."

"Can I help?" Susan offered. "What is it like?"

"There's no need for you to trouble, my dear."

He walked back to his wife's dressing-room and Tom took Susan by the arm and led her outside. His guileless old eyes smiled down at her gently. "Now don't you think any more about it," he said. "Put it right out of your mind."

"But it was horrible, Tom. Horrible."

"I know, my dear. Those stairs are a death-trap."

"Don't say that!"

"But it's true. If Maxine lives, it will be a miracle."

It wasn't until later that Susan remembered, not just his words, but the way in which he said them. Entirely without compassion; stating a bald fact which didn't seem to arouse any sadness in him.

They had reached the street door. Outside, the sun shone brilliantly. They paused for a moment before parting, and Philip Dunster came striding up the steps from the stage, behind them.

"Did you find your wife's bag?" Tom asked.

Philip patted his commodious brief-case. "Yes," he said. "I have it here." He nodded good-bye again, hailed a cruising taxi, and drove away.

The stage-doorkeeper caught Susan just as she was about to go. He was sorting mail — mostly Stephen's — and handed her a note.

"This is for you, miss. I found it buried in the H pigeon-hole."

Surprised, she took it. She never glanced at the pigeon-hole marked H because she was unaccustomed to receiving mail at the theatre, and always assumed that anything under H was for Stephen Hammond.

The note had been left by hand. It was nothing but a scrap of paper torn from a notebook and wrapped round her latch-key.

'Sorry, sweetie,' wrote Della in a hurry, 'but I seem to have walked off with

171

your key. You lent it to me last night, remember? I found it in my handbag and made Spike turn right round and bring me back. Don't wait up for me to-night. Spike has a pal who keeps a pub at Sonning; he's going to scrounge a meal for us there, so we'll probably be late . . . '

Susan pushed the key and the note into her handbag and walked the whole way home. She wanted air, but she also wanted to think. She was wondering why David had kept turning his attention to Maxine's fingers, and why he had said to her, beneath his breath, "Don't go out this afternoon. I want to talk to you. I'll come over." His voice had sounded urgent and her whole impression was that beneath his shock he was worried. So deeply worried that in another man it would have seemed like fear.

★ ★ ★

It was a surprise to discover, when she reached home, that the morning was by no means over. It gave her a sense of anticlimax, as if a curtain had forgotten to come down. The hours had to be filled in somehow, so she spent them cleaning her room, and after that she did Della's. By then it was lunch time, but she had no appetite. She cleaned the box-like kitchen instead, then washed her hair and her smalls, hanging bras and panties like bunting across the bathroom, her wet hair swathed turban-wise in a towel.

After that she plugged in Della's hair-drier and settled in front of it with a book, running her long fingers through her wet hair to let the warm air through. But she couldn't concentrate on reading. Two faces kept superimposing themselves across the printed page — Maxine's, and David's. Maxine's was chalk-white and very still, with a scarlet stain spreading from the back of her neck; a face that had lost all its beauty. David's was controlled, masking his thoughts, but somehow conveying a sense of deep inner conflict. But as well as the conflict there was something else. Alarm.

This alarm had conveyed itself to Susan like a disturbing undercurrent. David's reaction was more than that of a man shocked by an accident, more than the concern of a doctor for a seriously injured patient, and more than the emotion of a man finding his wife half dead. It was the naked alarm of someone who saw more than an accident behind the whole thing.

Susan's book slid unheeded to the floor. She sat very still, wondering if David actually believed that Maxine's fall was no tragic mischance, and if that was why he was coming to see her this afternoon; to talk about it, to tell her what he suspected, and why.

The sudden peal of the front-door bell made her leap to her feet, knocking the drier over. Her hands were trembling as she retrieved it, fumbled for the switch, and turned it off. She hadn't expected David yet, but she flew to the door to meet him, her damp hair flying.

Outside stood Ethel Fothergill.

"May I come in?" she said.

★ ★ ★

It was impossible to hide her surprise, so Susan made no attempt to. She held the door open, stammering a greeting, and Ethel said, "You weren't expecting me, of course."

The words weren't intended to be ambiguous, and there was no emphasis on the pronoun, but as soon as she had spoken, Ethel realised that Susan had mistaken her meaning.

"No," the girl answered without thinking. "I was expecting David," and in the circumstances it was natural for Ethel to wonder why. She wasn't aware of any particular friendship between those two, but the disappointment which underlay Susan's surprise was very obvious.

Nevertheless, her greeting was warm, and Ethel stepped into the tiny apartment feeling that at least she was welcome. That made things easier. She hadn't been looking forward to this visit, but obviously she and not Grace was the one to pay it. She was wondering how to lead up to the purpose of it when Susan said, "Would you like some coffee, or do you prefer tea?"

"I'm old-fashioned. A pot of tea appeals to me at any hour."

Susan flashed a smile, the mouth

curving sweetly, the teeth very white, the eyes frank and friendly. Ethel thought her one of the nicest girls she had met for a long time and that if David Radcliffe had fallen in love with her she didn't blame him, although it was unfortunate that he had met Maxine first.

The thought of Maxine brought Ethel back to her visit, and the reason for it. A perfectly simple request should be easy to make, but somehow she wasn't finding it so. She knew that Susan must be wondering why she had come, and was waiting to be told. Meanwhile, with a rather touching shyness, the girl was doing her best to be a good hostess.

To a fledgling straight from drama school, Ethel Fothergill was a big name, a renowned character actress of whom even the critics spoke with respect. Only one thing would have surprised Susan more than a visit from Ethel Fothergill, and that would have been a visit from Grace Challoner.

In the theatrical world there was a wide division between leading players and under-studies. Outside it, social levels might have begun to even out, but

176

within it was a hierarchy into which one was only accepted after distinguished experience. Even a sudden leap to fame had to be based on real artistic merit to qualify for membership.

In the circumstances it was obvious that Ethel's visit must have a specific reason. They had exchanged no more than greetings at rehearsals; they were virtually strangers, so Susan also guessed that Ethel had gone out of her way to find out her address.

As Susan busied herself in the box of a kitchen, Ethel looked around. The small sitting-room was obviously converted into a bedroom at night, the divan couch bright with cheap scatter cushions and the bookshelves along one wall housing an extensive and well-chosen selection of paperbacks. There was a photograph of a middle-aged couple whom Ethel took to be Susan's parents, a kindly, homely couple from the look of them. Ethel wondered how they felt about having a talented daughter, if they realised how outstanding her talent really was and, if so, whether they were surprised, proud, or merely bewildered by it.

Susan returned with a tray. The cups didn't match, but, like the room, were gay and cheerful.

"None of our china matches," she confessed without embarrassment, "so we call it our harlequin set. Della and I — she's the girl I live with — went round the market stalls picking up rejects when we furnished this place. We had to do it on a shoe-string — at least, I did, so Della pitched in with the same amount." A dimple quivered at the corner of her mouth. "I think her parents were surprised. They're rich, you see, so of course they've no idea just how far a few pounds *can* be made to stretch."

"And your parents? What did they think?"

"The same as I — that a team-up between a girl accustomed to unlimited money and one accustomed to very little just wouldn't work out. We come from very different backgrounds, you see."

I'm chatting too much, Susan thought wildly, and wondered why Ethel Fothergill was letting her run on so. It didn't occur to her that the woman was glad to let her, or that she, in turn, was nervous.

"There goes the kettle!" Susan said thankfully, rushing back to the kitchen in response to a high-pitched whistle.

This is ridiculous, thought Ethel, half ashamed, and it's unkind of me to keep the poor child in suspense.

She resolved to come to the point as quickly as possible and get away. She had a lot to do before the early performance this evening and time was marching on.

In the kitchen Susan glanced at her watch and saw that it was two-thirty. She wondered what time David would arrive and hoped that Ethel Fothergill would have left by then, although his call could easily be attributed to an anxiety to find out how she felt after the morning's shock.

As if sensing her thoughts, Ethel said as Susan re-entered the room, "You must have had a terrible shock this morning, finding my niece like that."

It was an opening gambit, leading up to the reason for her visit, and Susan was intelligent enough to recognise it as such. She poured the tea carefully before answering.

"The shock must have been worse for

Doctor Radcliffe. He is her husband."

"Of course. All the same, to a sensitive girl such a sight could be unnerving."

"I come from a tough Northern town, Miss Fothergill. I don't faint at the sight of blood."

The words were not insolent, but they did say, Come to the point — I don't believe it is concern for me that brought you here.

Touché, thought Ethel, and smiled, but even so she still found it difficult to put a bald question. Suddenly Susan made it easier for her by asking, with straight-from-the-shoulder Northern candour, "Was there anything you wanted to ask me — about the accident, I mean? Being Miss Culver's aunt I suppose you would like details, but for those I think you should contact Doctor Radcliffe, or the hospital."

"I telephoned the hospital. Doctor Radcliffe wasn't available and they could give me no information about my niece, as yet."

"That must be worrying for you."

"Naturally, I am upset about such a thing happening, but I must confess that

180

this isn't wholly due to the fact that the victim was Maxine. Although she is my niece, we were never very close."

"The victim?" Susan echoed, a little startled.

"How else does one refer to someone involved in an accident? The victim of a road crash or an accident of any kind is still a victim."

"Of course."

Another uncomfortable pause. Susan took Ethel's cup and refilled it.

"Is there anything you want to ask me? Anything you want me to do?"

"Only give me her handbag," Ethel said a shade too casually.

14

SO there it was, out at last, a
perfectly simple request which had
been perfectly simple to make, and
promptly Ethel felt relieved.

Susan had an unaccountable desire to
laugh. All this fencing and hedging just
for that!

"I haven't got it," she admitted. "I
handed it in at the hospital on my way
home."

Ethel was silent and remained so, all
her skill as an actress carefully masking
her reaction.

"You didn't want it particularly, did
you, Miss Fothergill?"

"No, my dear. I just thought that I
should go along to her flat and get some
things for her. Night attire. That sort of
thing. Her key would be in her bag."

"I shouldn't worry about that and I
shouldn't think she'll need night attire.
She'll be wearing surgical clothing."

"Of course."

The woman's voice was tight and controlled. Susan looked at her and said with compassion, "Try not to worry too much. St. Bede's is a wonderful hospital and she couldn't be in better hands. I can understand your wanting to do something, of course, and the awful thing is not being able to. I remember my mother feeling that way when Dad was rushed off with pneumonia. She felt helpless and frustrated and desperately worried, and being unable to do a thing for him made it so much worse for her."

Ethel managed a smile. "I thought young people nowadays were supposed to have no feelings. Now I know it isn't true. You're very sympathetic and understanding, my dear."

Susan didn't know what to say to that, so she fell back on renewed reassurances about the hospital and added, with a confidence she did not feel, that she was sure Maxine would pull through.

"I hope so, although from the sound of things her injuries must have been severe."

And where did she hear that, Susan wondered.

"Grace Challoner telephoned me," Ethel said as if in explanation. "Her husband gave her what details he could."

"I see."

The visit had come to an unsatisfactory and inconclusive end and there was nothing for Ethel to do but get up and go. She said good-bye, thanked Susan for the tea and sympathy, and departed.

At the door she said unexpectedly, "They say it's an ill wind that blows no one some good, so at least you will benefit."

Startled, Susan replied, "I don't understand."

"I mean that you will get the part now."

"I hadn't even thought about that!"

Ethel saw two high spots of colour in the girl's cheeks, and said hastily, "Of course, you hadn't thought about it. Forgive me."

Her smile was gentle and rather sad. Susan shut the door, feeling obscurely sorry for her, although she couldn't really analyse why. It had been plain at the theatre that there was no love lost between aunt and niece, and Ethel had implied as much just now. Therefore her carefully controlled anxiety struck an unconvincing and faintly puzzling note.

* * *

David arrived about half an hour later. Susan was giving a final rub to her hair with a towel.

"Sorry I haven't had time to glam up for you," she said, and he laughed. It seemed to him that it was the first time he had laughed for a long time.

"I like you that way."

"Have you eaten? If not, I can knock something up."

"Have *you* eaten?"

"I wasn't hungry, but I did have a cup of tea with Ethel Fothergill."

"Ethel Fothergill?" he echoed in surprise. "Has she been here?"

"She called for Maxine's handbag. She wanted to go along to her flat to get some things for her, so needed her latch-key."

"Maxine won't need anything more than the hospital provides, for a long time to come."

Susan said quietly, "It's serious, isn't it?"

"Severe spinal and brain injuries. Her condition is critical." His voice was taut. "To be honest, it is only a question of time. No one could survive for long in such a condition."

"Oh, David, how terrible. I'm sorry."

To Susan's ears the words sounded trite and inadequate, but her distress was deep and David sensed it. He took hold of her hands.

"You know I didn't love her any more, but God knows I wouldn't have wanted this to happen to her. Come and sit down. I must talk to you."

She said firmly, "When you've had some coffee. You need it."

She had never seen a man so white and strained. It was more than shock, more than concern, more than the fearful realisation that the woman he was married to was going to die.

To her surprise, David did as he was told. When she returned with the coffee he was sitting on the couch with his head in his hands. He looked up at her, dragging his hands down his face as if wiping away his thoughts. He accepted the coffee silently, and drank it. He even ate the sandwiches she put before him, but he was hardly aware of what he did. Then Susan said, "You're terribly worried, I can tell."

"Then you can also tell that I'm not just worried about the accident itself, but about the way it happened."

"I don't understand."

"It's her fingers. They were damaged in a way that couldn't only be due to the fall. If she had grabbed at the iron steps as she catapulted down, or if she had hung on to the edge to break her fall, the underside of her fingers would have suffered the worst. They would have been torn and bleeding. But they are damaged on top, as well."

"But how?"

"They were crushed," David answered.

Susan felt sick. Apprehension filled her like a slowly spreading nausea. She knew what he meant and that he didn't want to put it into words, so she clutched at a straw and said, "You mean — as if they'd been trapped somehow? In a cupboard, or a drawer . . . ?"

"Worse than that. Hammered on. Or stamped on."

"*Stamped* on?"

"Yes. Someone either struck her fingers repeatedly, or stamped on them as she hung on to the side of the iron steps. Someone who was determined to make her fall to her death."

15

THEY sat for a long time, talking about it, going over and over and round and round and always coming back full circle. The plain facts were that Maxine had fallen down the central well of the spiral staircase, and in the course of her fall her body struck hard projections at varied intervals — "The iron steps, of course, if at that stage she was tumbling down the stairs following the circular construction," said David, "but after that she had taken one violent drop, and somewhere along the route her fingers had been crushed."

Shocked, Susan asked, "Will it be necessary to notify the police?"

"If she dies, it may well be, unless we can establish that the damage to her fingers was not deliberately inflicted. If by some miracle she recovers consciousness — and miracles *have* been known to happen — she may remember a few details. If there is a perfectly simple explanation for the crushed fingers — that they were trapped in a door or a cupboard, as you suggest, before the accident took place — then there can be no suggestion of foul play, but if not, yes, police will have to be notified. The question is, how long can we stall?"

"Stall? I don't understand. Why stall?"

"Because I want to find out how it happened, and if anyone else was involved, and how, and why. Otherwise, I am the obvious suspect."

"I don't see why!" Susan protested.

David smiled and touched her cheek gratefully.

"You don't, but the police would. Who would benefit most from Maxine's death? *I* would, and I don't mean materially. I had left her long ago, begged for a divorce, wanted to be rid of her, and even so recently as yesterday had refused ever to go back to her. That's the simple truth. She suggested a reconciliation only last Tuesday, on the morning of the first rehearsal, and despite the way I felt I went away and thought the whole thing over. I stared every fact in the face, argued for and against and mostly against, and then I went back to the theatre yesterday to tell her my decision. It may surprise you to know what it was — to do as she suggested. Why I decided this I can't say, except that she was still my wife and I felt it my duty to have one last try at making a success of things. Maybe it's just the way I've been brought up — full of middle-class ideas that many people scorn, ideas about duty and sticking to one's bargains. Anyway, despite the fact that I knew I didn't love her any more and that there wasn't the slightest chance of my ever doing so again, I thought it was the *right* thing to do — to try to salvage something out of our marriage, even if it was only companionship. So I went along to the theatre to tell her."

"And — you told her?"

"No. She weighed right in by being bitchy. She showed every mean characteristic that had ever disgusted me, and I knew she would never change and that our marriage would never change. To start again would merely be to start as before, the whole horrible relationship repeating itself. And suddenly I said no. Not now or ever, I told her. And she said, 'That's a pity, because not now or ever will you be free of me. Just try to get rid of me — *if* you can.'"

"But no one knew about this! No one heard!"

"Tom Langley did. Suddenly we looked up and there he was, calling her to the telephone. He'd tiptoed along the row because Grace and Stephen were rehearsing. How long he'd been there, I don't know — perhaps only a minute. But it was long enough for him to hear what she said."

Susan was sitting at David's feet. Her hands were clasped in his, an unconscious gesture answering an instinctive need. She said reassuringly, "No one could possibly suspect you. For one thing, you weren't in the theatre this morning. Not when it happened, anyway. You arrived just before I came back — "

"Came back?"

"Yes. I'd arrived much too early. No one was there, so I went for a walk and a cup of coffee — "

"Did you see anyone back-stage?"

"Not a soul. Everywhere was in

complete darkness and the iron curtain was still down. I was the first to arrive. But it was funny . . . " Her voice tailed away uncertainly.

"What was funny?"

"A feeling I had. Just a feeling. As if I wasn't alone."

David's hands tightened on hers. He didn't like to remind her that she had probably not been alone, that someone must have been lurking in the shadows, that even then Maxine's unconscious body lay beneath the spiral staircase.

"Is it possible to tell when the accident actually happened?" Susan asked.

"Pretty well. Examination pin-pointed it to about half an hour before we found her."

"Then — she was there all the time! It happened even before I arrived!"

"Yes."

"So — if — if someone *did* — "

"They must have been there, too."

She remembered the feeling that a door had been silently shut. She remembered Philip Dunster emerging from his wife's dressing-room when she returned. She looked at David with startled eyes and said, "*Philip Dunster?*"

"I've thought of him, but it doesn't make sense. What reason could he have? As far as I'm aware, they didn't even know each other. Not that that is anything to go by. Maxine had many friends with whom I was totally unacquainted, even when we lived together. All the same, it's hard to believe that a man like him, married to a woman like Grace . . . "

"I know what you mean. He's too — too *nice*. And too happily married."

David thought of all the apparently happy couples he had known or heard of, whose private lives had proved to be startling and unexpected. He had done a lot of thinking since Maxine's accident — desperate, frantic thinking, scouring every avenue, exploring every channel, and always coming back to one glaring fact. That the person with the strongest reason for wishing Maxine dead was himself.

"There must have been some logical explanation for Dunster visiting the theatre in his wife's absence," David said thoughtfully.

"There was. He had come to collect

194

her handbag. He said she left it the night before. But the funny thing was that he'd picked up the wrong one."

"What do you mean?"

"I mean that he had picked up Maxine's."

"*Maxine*'s? Are you sure?"

"Quite sure. After you had gone in the ambulance I offered to take care of it. He handed it over, saying he had mistaken it for his wife's, but I should have thought that a man would have known what his wife's handbag looked like."

"That depends on how many she had. With all her money, Grace probably has a lot. What worries me more is *where* Dunster picked it up — in his wife's dressing-room, or on the floor beside Maxine. That's the important thing."

"But what motive could he have for taking the bag if he knew it was Maxine's?"

"That," said David decisively, "is what I mean to find out."

All along he had felt that Maxine had forced Grace into giving her the part of Nina. Now he was convinced of it. She had blackmailed the woman, and a clue to that blackmail would very probably be in her handbag. It was logical to assume that she would keep such evidence very close in her possession.

And now Ethel Fothergill had visited Susan, also asking for the bag.

"What did you do with it?" David asked suddenly.

"I handed it in at the hospital."

He planted a hearty kiss on her forehead.

"Bless you!" he cried. "I'm going back there right away."

"David — "

"Yes?"

"Ethel Fothergill said something that worried me, something I didn't like. That proverb about an ill wind blowing somebody some good. She meant me."

"*You?*"

"I'll get the part now, she said. I didn't like the implication."

"My dear, there could be no implication. You — of all people!"

"She said she didn't mean it that way, and I'm sure she didn't. She's a nice woman, and I trust her. All the same, I didn't like it."

196

Very gently, David put his arms about her. He held her like a child in need of comfort. Against his shoulder, she said with a little choke, "I don't like *this*, either! I don't want to be comforted like a child. I'm a woman."

As if I didn't know, he thought, putting her very firmly aside.

* * *

Maxine had been put in an isolation ward, where she hovered perilously on the brink of life and death. She had been in a coma when David left the hospital, she was still in a coma when he returned. The resident surgical officer, who had taken charge of the case on admission, was still with her. So were a sister and staff nurse.

She could linger like this for hours, even days, the R.S.O. told him in a low voice, and a major operation could prove fatal. Her heart had to be brought to the required condition for that; it had been seriously damaged through shock. Meanwhile, all urgent attention had been carried out, and the only thing now left

197

to do was to help her turn the corner. After that, the battle for full recovery could begin.

It was all a question of waiting, and hoping, and fighting. They told him this as they would have told a grief-stricken relative, because that was what they expected him to be. He felt ashamed that his strongest emotion was horror. The sight of her battered body made David react as all forms of suffering made him react, filling him with a desperate desire to alleviate it. It was this compassion which now made him view his wife's ashen face with the deepest pity he had ever felt for her.

But pity wasn't love, and he was too honest to pretend. He saw the sister's eyes upon him, searching for some sign of a husband's grief, but all he could reveal was this appalling pity.

Maxine looked a stranger to him, lying there with a face as white as the bandages about her head. The face had Maxine's features — the straight, chiselled nose, the arched eyebrows, the fine bone structure which, he had thought when he first fell in love with her, made her one of the most beautiful young women he had ever met, but now, stripped of its make-up and bereft of any sign of life, it was a pallid mask with thin lips on which no tenderness or passion had ever been traced.

A detached corner of his mind recalled how carefully she had painted those lips, softening them into curves which nature had not bestowed, erasing the thin cruelty, the petty meanness, the cold selfishness. Experience had since convinced him that a person's mouth revealed more of their character than any other feature, with the exception of the eyes. These, in his wife's case, had been beautiful and she had skilfully made them even more so, but, like the mouth, they had also been cold by nature.

It was hard to recall the passionate adoration he had once felt for her, the wild desire, the besotted devotion, but that was the way in which he had fallen in love with her as a young and impressionable student. It had been a whirlwind affair, flaring like a fire and dying just as quickly, fanned by the exciting contrast she made with the life and people he had known. The tragedy of it was that he had married her before the fire had burned itself out.

He stood beside her bed, acknowledging the R.S.O.'s comments with an occasional nod, only half listening to what the man said. David knew the medical details, anyway. He had heard them before he left the hospital and they confirmed his own conclusions. Now he studied her nearly lifeless form with a kind of incredulous disbelief, wondering why it was so difficult to recall what she had been like when animated and alive. Now she had acquired a strange remoteness, like a figure in a trance, unreachable, beyond communication, and yet she lived and breathed and the heart in her body, faint and scarcely detectable, still functioned enough to sustain the tenuous thread of her life.

The R.S.O. said, "Try not to worry. We're doing all we can," and left David alone with the nurses. If the staff had been surprised to learn that this woman was his wife, not once had they shown it. From the moment that David had arrived with her in the ambulance, traditional detachment had marked the faces of the hospital staff. It marked Sister's face right at this moment, even though she was wondering just how the nurses had reacted to the news that young Doctor Radcliffe was married. Everyone regarded him as one of the most eligible men in the hospital, so she could guess what a stir it had made on the wards. By now it was probably the chief topic of conversation in the nurses' home.

David glanced at the locker beside his wife's bed. There was nothing there but a carafe of water, which struck him as ironical since she was in no condition to drink it. Sister noticed his glance and said, "That carafe can be moved, Staff Nurse," and the girl picked it up and went outside.

"Is there anything you want to ask me, Doctor?"

She was a middle-aged woman with a kindly but inquisitive face. She was new to St. Bede's, but since her arrival she believed she had found out all she wanted to know about the medical staff — how many were married and if any were having affairs with the nurses, which meant that *she* would put a stop to all that. The fact that David Radcliffe was one of the youngest doctors and certainly the most attractive had made her assume, right at the beginning, that he needed watching. It had astonished her to find that she was wrong. For a man with very evident sex appeal, it was strange that he was involved with none of the nursing staff, nor was he ever caught flirting with them when off duty. But now she knew why. Secretly, he had been married all along, which meant that many a nurse's hopes had gone crashing during the last few hours.

David said frankly, "I was looking for my wife's hand-bag. Very stupidly, I've mislaid my latch-key and will have to take hers."

He looked tired and he sounded tired and sister didn't blame him for wanting to get home. Her heart was touched with pity for him. She imagined him returning to an empty house, desolate and lonely.

She opened the locker and took out Maxine's bag and gave it to him, saying, "Isn't there anyone you can go to to-night? I really wouldn't advise

202

you to be alone. Have you no relatives to look after you?"

"I'll be all right, Sister. Thank you, all the same."

The door opened and staff nurse re-entered. Sister gave her some instructions, then turned back to David and said, "Well, I'll be on my rounds, Doctor, if there's nothing I can do for you."

He shook his head, thanking her, but wishing she would go. She gave him a sympathetic smile.

"Try not to worry, Doctor. I should get a good night's sleep, if I were you."

The door closed behind her. The staff nurse sat down at a table and stooped over Maxine's chart. Her back was to David, so he walked out of the room, taking the handbag with him.

Half-way down the corridor he turned into the men's cloakroom. Luckily, it was empty. He examined the contents of Maxine's handbag quickly. It was cluttered and, contrary to the immaculate suède exterior, dusty with face powder, smudged with lipstick — messy, like her own personality beneath her outward elegance. There were a couple of combs, one broken, the other full of hairs, and both slightly dirty; a rather gaudy powder compact, a handkerchief impregnated with spilled face powder; two or three lipsticks; mascara; old bus tickets and bits of paper; tatty bills. There were no personal letters, but one of the bills bore her address, so he took it. He also took the only key the bag contained, obviously a latch-key, then turned his attention to the zipped centre pocket, which revealed a quantity of loose change and a note-case. Inside the note-case were some postage stamps, membership cards for a couple of Soho drinking clubs, five separate pound notes and one ten-shilling. He was about to thrust the note-case back when he saw, carefully inserted between the pound notes, a newspaper cutting.

Footsteps sounded in the corridor outside, jerking him to attention. He was relieved when they passed the door. He pushed the newspaper cutting into his jacket pocket, closed the handbag, walked back to Maxine's room, and went inside.

The staff nurse was still working on the chart, which meant that he couldn't have been away for more than a couple of minutes. He smiled at the girl and said, "Stupid of me, I went off with my wife's handbag. All I wanted was a latch-key."

He gave the bag to the staff nurse, and went away.

16

HE read the newspaper cutting as he drove to Bayswater in a taxi. It was brief and meant nothing to him, except that if his wife knew the people concerned, she had some pretty shabby friends. That didn't surprise him. In the past it had not been unusual for him to come home to find unpleasant characters cluttering up the flat; men who made him feel an intruder in his own home; women who blatantly offered themselves, but whom he wouldn't even touch.

Maxine thought he was a prude, and said so.

"They're fun, darling! They're individuals, people who have the courage to live as they want to live. Not dull suburban types exactly like their neighbours."

But these 'courageous' individuals treated his home like a club and helped his wife to run up drink bills which he, the dull suburban type, was left to pay.

Recalling the past served no useful purpose now. Resentment was as destructive an emotion as hatred, so he thrust it aside. Idly, he glanced at the bill which had provided him with Maxine's address. It was a final demand for a sum far more than she could afford to run up on the not ungenerous allowance he made her. She had always had expensive tastes. Apparently she still had. The bill was for clothes from a pricey Knightsbridge store.

But her address didn't come up to the same expensive standard. It was a shabby side street bordering on Paddington; a tall, dilapidated Victorian house with peeling plaster and a crumbling portico, a tragic remnant of long-lost elegance.

Beside the front door, which had not seen a lick of paint for many a year, a variety of names were displayed in a variety of ways. Bits of paper and tattered pieces of card were stuck beneath bell-pushes, or fixed to the woodwork with drawing pins. Only one made any claim to elegance, a small engraved copper plate bearing Maxine's name, Flat 8, third floor.

The main door was half-open and led into a musty hall from which stairs covered in worn linoleum led down to a gloomy basement. Two doors opened from the ground floor. These were to flats numbers one and two. Outside the first was a soiled perambulator and a bicycle; outside the other a pail of rubbish. The pattern was more or less repeated on the next two floors, but the third was slightly better. Nothing was dumped outside Maxine's door and her immediate neighbour's displayed nothing more offensive than a row of dirty milk bottles which looked as if they had been there for a long time and would remain for a long time yet.

The latch-key from Maxine's handbag admitted him to a glorified bed-sitting-room in a state of complete confusion. She had always been untidy, but this was worse even than the old days. Ashtrays overflowed. Dirty tumblers stood forgotten. Clothes hung from the picture rail and over chairs. The bed was unmade and the atmosphere was laden with stale cigarette smoke, yesterday's cooking, and tired perfume.

David felt a sense of disgust. Now he understood why Maxine had been so anxious to come back to him. She had never lived at this squalid standard as his wife, untidy and undomesticated though she had been. Even as a medical student the two-roomed flat he had managed to provide in the less expensive part of Blackheath had been better than this. This place was a dump in which someone very badly off lived, ate, slept and drank in unfriendly solitude.

He had pitied Maxine at the hospital. Now he pitied her even more if this was all she had been able to achieve, even with the aid of the monthly allowance he paid by banker's order into her account. That alone, he thought as he looked around, should have maintained a better standard of living than this.

He picked up a dress lying negligently over a chair. He didn't know much about women's clothes, but his short marriage had taught him to recognise the cheap from the expensive in his wife's wardrobe, and this dress was certainly expensive. Material, cut, workmanship, and the name of the couture house, substantiated this. Shoes kicked off at random bore the stamp of hand-made Italian craftsmanship.

There were clothes everywhere, mutely testifying that this was how Maxine spent her money, piling it on her back and economising on her standard of living. It was an undignified way of life, but it was her choice.

He glanced at a litter of bills on a dusty desk. Most were for clothing and cosmetics, a few for wines and spirits, none for groceries. The none-too-clean cupboard which served as a larder — the kitchen didn't even boast a modest fridge — contained a few items of tinned food, half a loaf in a crumby tin, a packet of tea, and a half-empty tin of coffee. Nothing else.

Crockery was cheap and chipped. There was very little of it, but what there was was stacked in the sink, suggesting that a piece was taken out when needed, rinsed, used and dumped back again. The curtains were black with London smoke and horrible to the touch.

The whole place was depressing and David regretted coming. He even began to wonder why he had done so, then remembered that his object had been to search for evidence of blackmail. The very thought now made him smile. If Maxine had sunk to that practice she showed little sign of profiting by it, apart from her lavish wardrobe, and the spoils of blackmail would have brought her more than that.

He also knew her well enough to be aware that she would never save a penny, and this was confirmed when he came across her bank pass book in a drawer. It was heavily in the red. He also found a letter from her bank manager asking her to call at an early date to discuss the question of her overdraft 'which is now in excess of the agreed figure.'

Precisely when he began to feel that someone else had gone through the place before him David really couldn't tell, but suddenly he suspected that other hands had searched through her drawers and that not even Maxine, allowing for a deterioration in her already haphazard habits, would leave her things in such chaotic disorder as this.

The suspicion became conviction when

he found every handbag she possessed half-emptied on the bed, contents strewn, the handbags thrown aside.

Someone in a hurry had searched, discarded, and searched again. Other hands had rummaged through untidy drawers and emptied pigeon-holes, thrusting the contents back. Suitcases had been opened and pushed impatiently aside. Whoever had been here before him had added to the original confusion, not attempting to cover their tracks. So the logical thing to conclude was that the search had been made by someone who knew that Maxine was not coming back.

He cast one last glance about the room, realising that it was a waste of time to search for something which he could not even identify because he had no idea what he was really looking for, and in view of the fact that he had come across nothing which struck him as odd, or unusual, or implicated anyone whose name was familiar to him, he gave up the fruitless search and left.

Downstairs, he found the caretaker in the basement. From the state of the place, and of herself, he wondered what precisely she took care of. She was a slut of a woman with a cigarette dangling untidily from one corner of her mouth. She didn't trouble to remove the cigarette as she talked, and when ash spilled down the front of a stained overall she didn't even notice.

Had anyone called on Miss Culver in flat number eight? Well, maybe they'd 'ad and maybe they 'adn't, 'ow was she to know? *She* 'ad more to do than spy on the tenants' goings-on. 'Sides, she was stuck-up, that one, all la-di-da and pretending she was an actress, but when she'd last acted, 'eaven only knew. Liked to think she was better'n everyone else in the 'ouse, with her swanky brass plate by the doorbell 'n' all.

David checked an impulse to turn on his heel. He fingered his wallet instead.

The tune changed immediately.

"Well, now, sir, maybe I *can* remember someone coming, but only 'cos I 'appened to be around, mind you. Said Miss Culver'd met with an accident or something and was in 'ospital, wouldya believe it, so she'd come to get some things for 'er . . . "

"She?"

"Elderly lady, she was. A bit 'oity-toity-like, but nicer'n 'er niece. Oh, yes, that's wot she said she was — Miss Culver's aunt. Surprised me. Didn't know that one 'ad any relatives! Well, *thank* you, sir — if there's anything else you'd like to know . . . "

He didn't bother to reply. Somehow he had guessed that Ethel Fothergill had been here before him, coming straight from Susan's place after failing to recover the handbag, taking a chance on finding someone to let her into Maxine's flat.

He had reached the top of the basement steps when the caretaker's voice came after him.

"Oh, there *was* one thing I forgot, sir — the lady wasn't alone. A man was with 'er. I forgot about this 'cos 'e waited for 'er outside and I didn't see 'im until she left."

"What was he like?"

"Well, I couldn't see 'im clearly, mind, seeing as 'ow 'e was in the taxi. It must've bin tickin' up like mad, though she was only up there a few minutes packin' a bag."

214

"But you caught a glimpse of him?"

The woman hesitated, calculating whether an additional price could be fixed for additional information, then deciding that here was a customer not to be played about with. Besides, she hadn't done too badly already.

"Well, only a glimpse, mind you. Old, 'e was, and sort've funny."

"Funny?"

"Odd. Different. *You* know wot I mean. Arty-like, with an overcoat over 'is shoulders like a cloak and the brim of 'is 'at turned up more one side than the other, like . . . like . . . "

Like an Edwardian actor. Like old Tom Langley.

David wasn't surprised. If Ethel had not known her niece's address she could have got it from him. As well as being stage director, Tom helped Grace on the managerial side and had access to all cast details. In this instance he had gone one step further, helping Ethel in a time of shock by taking her to her niece's address.

They're a clan, David thought. A close-knit, loyal little clan, helping and protecting one another. Ethel, Tom, Grace, Stephen — and Philip Dunster, too. They had built the Comet Theatre Company together and they would stick together.

But if one of them had tried to kill Maxine, how strong would their loyalty be?

David went straight to the theatre, determined to find out. It was then a quarter to six, which meant that the curtain had already risen on Saturday's early performance.

17

GRACE CHALLONER removed her street make-up carefully. In the glare of naked electric bulbs surrounding her dressingroom mirror she saw Ethel Fothergill's face framed like a portrait in a glassy pool.

"I didn't find a thing," Ethel was saying. "The place was a shambles and even worse when I left. It hardly seemed necessary to hide the fact that I'd been searching — all I did was to increase the general untidiness." She ran a tired hand across her forehead, pushing back a strand of grey hair. "I can't understand how my sister ever came to have a daughter like Maxine. Ruth was one of the gentlest, sweetest and calmest people I've ever known. Of course, Keith was a devil — quite unscrupulous — but his personality was so strong that it could influence anyone for a while. He swept poor Ruth off her feet, and even after she married him she would never admit that she'd made a mistake. I'm sure it was his influence which turned Maxine into the person she is."

"Plus inheriting a few of his characteristics, I imagine. There doesn't seem to have been much of her mother in her."

"Ruth died when Maxine was in her early teens. Sometimes I think that was a good thing, and sometimes I don't. Had she lived, her influence might have counteracted Keith's. On the other hand, her heart might have been broken between the pair of them. Keith's cunning didn't get him anywhere in the end, and as for Maxine — " Ethel's shoulders lifted in a despairing shrug. "Well, we know how she turned out."

"Will she live?" Grace asked. "God knows, I've every reason to wish the girl out of the way, but not that way. Just out of all our lives, making no more trouble."

"Well, she can't make trouble for a long time yet, placed as she is. What puzzles me is what she was *doing* in the theatre this morning. There was no rehearsal call for the principals, only the under-studies, so not a single member of the cast had any reason to be there, and Tom tells me he didn't arrive until after David and Susan had found her."

"And Philip before them. He dropped in to collect my handbag in passing."

Ethel said with feeling. "What a pity he didn't take Maxine's! I'm pretty sure the remainder of that newspaper cutting would be in it. She'd never let it out of her sight. Well, I must get ready. The half-hour call will be coming shortly."

It came at that moment, vibrating over the Tannoy.

Ethel didn't make her entrance until long after Grace, so it wasn't essential for her to be made up and ready by the time the curtain went up.

"I'll be thankful when this show comes off," Grace said. "Only one more week, thank heaven, and then we can concentrate on rehearsals for *Wings of Morning*. I hope that play isn't going to be ill-starred."

"It won't be," Ethel said comfortingly. "It's a good play, and with Maxine out of it everyone will be a great deal happier. I'm afraid I rather upset Susan Howard when I called on her this afternoon. I said that at least Maxine's accident ensured her getting the part now, which was a tactless remark to make. She's a sensitive child."

"And a nice one. Has the hospital issued a bulletin yet?"

"Not that I've heard, but I'll go along between this show and the late one. If they'll let me see her, I may be able to get hold of her bag."

Grace put out a hand and touched the woman's sleeve gratefully.

"You've done enough. I've bothered you enough. Philip said I was to leave everything to him. Now let's do that. Ring the hospital for news of Maxine, if you're really anxious, but try not to worry. I'm sure she'll pull through . . . "

Ethel said frankly, "Let's be honest, shall we? There isn't a person amongst us who wouldn't be glad to see the last of Maxine. I don't suppose any of us would really wish her dead, but who would actually weep if it happened? Not even me, her aunt. All I would feel would be sorrow that such a thing should happen to my sister's child."

She spoke the truth and now that it had

been aired, it brought a relief of tension. It was no use pretending. Maxine had been a menace to her aunt's security and to Grace's happiness. She couldn't have made David Radcliffe happy, either, thought Grace wryly, so that was three people who had no cause to mourn her death. Add Philip to these and you had four. Add Susan Howard, who also had good reason for wishing her out of the way, and there were five.

When Grace came off-stage at the end of the first act, Philip was waiting in her dressing-room. When the door closed he took her in his arms and held her close. She relaxed against him, only now fully aware of the effort it had been to act with her customary serenity. She had moved and walked and talked on stage like an automaton, sustained by Stephen Hammond's performance and her own professionalism, but she wanted nothing so much as to go home with Philip and shut the door upon the world.

But if the story of herself and Lew Martin became known, the world would be clamouring for admittance. Press, radio, television, all the merciless tentacles which probed into one's personal life, would do their worst.

She shuddered a little, and Philip said gently, "I can't find out a thing until I go to Australia House on Monday and search their newspaper files. They keep the *Sydney Morning Herald* for years back. I *could* make discreet enquiries through the Home Office, but I'd rather do that in a routine way on a routine week-day than attract attention or arouse curiosity at the week-end, so we'll just have to possess our souls in patience and thank heaven that Maxine can make no mischief now. In the meantime, if we can lay our hands on the rest of that cutting, we can at least destroy it and stop worrying on that score until I find out what has happened to Lew Martin."

"Philip — when you had gone out after lunch I asked Ethel to see if she could get hold of Maxine's handbag. As her relative I thought the hospital might allow her to see her, but they wouldn't. No visitors, except her husband. So then she went along to see Susan Howard."

"You didn't tell Ethel that I had

handed the bag over to her?"

"No, merely that I understood from Tom that Susan had taken it. That's true, anyway. Tom did mention it in passing when I talked to him on the phone, so I was able to pass on the information quite naturally. In any case, Ethel herself said that it was a pity you couldn't have got hold of it when you called to collect mine. She believes that really is why you were at the theatre."

"Good. We must stick to that. No one knows, except you and me, that I telephoned Maxine and arranged to meet her here at ten-thirty-five this morning. Also, no one except you and me knows that I picked up her handbag from the floor, and that's the way it must remain."

"I understand."

"The only thing I can do before Monday is to search Maxine's flat, if I can gain admittance."

"Ethel has done that. There wasn't a trace of the cutting."

There was a tap on the door, and Grace's dresser entered with a tray of tea. Hard on the woman's heels came Stephen

Hammond, looking shocked, although he tried to cover it up, as he tried to cover all his nervous tension lately.

"What's all this about Maxine? I only arrived a quarter of an hour before the curtain went up and didn't hear a thing until now. Tom told me as I came off-stage. Why didn't you tell me before we went on, Grace? We were standing in the wings waiting for our cue together for at least a couple of minutes before the curtain went up."

Grace said with truth, "It didn't occur to me that you hadn't heard."

"How did it happen?"

"She fell down the spiral staircase."

"What was she doing there? Early on a Saturday morning, too, when no one was around."

"Which is precisely what no one knows," Philip told him, accepting a cup of tea from Grace.

"It's horrible!" Stephen shuddered. "There hasn't been an accident like this at the Comet since we took it over. Tom tells me she's seriously injured. How seriously?"

"Critically."

"Then she must have fallen from a good height. That means one of the top floors, doesn't it? But those are reserved for male members of the company, like myself and Tom . . . "

"We don't know from what height she fell, but pitching down on to that floor even from a moderate height could cause a lot of injury," Philip said. "Part of it is stone, where the big doors open at the side to admit scenery, and that extends as far as the base of the stairs."

"Do you really think it was an accident?" Stephen asked.

Grace put down her cup with a sharp little clatter.

"*Not* an accident? What else could it be?"

"Someone might have tried to bump her off," Stephen said brashly. "I should think every one of us hated her guts."

"She wasn't popular, but none of us would have wanted to murder her!"

Stephen said with bravado, "Well, *I* did, on more than one occasion, and everyone knows it!"

Grace dismissed that with a laugh.

"No one took you seriously. Why should they? How many times does the average person declare that they could murder someone who exasperates them? It's a very common figure of speech. One has to have a bigger motive for murder than exasperation."

Philip said nothing. He was remembering a piece of information given him by the Commissioner of Scotland Yard at a dinner party one night — that at least half of convicted murderers appear to have no motive, and that when there was a motive it proved to be the most paltry and unimportant circumstance in the majority of cases.

"We are talking of the girl in the past tense already," Stephen said with a touch of shame. "But she will get better, won't she?"

"We can only hope so," Grace answered, thinking how much more honest it would be to admit that one didn't.

Somehow, she got through the rest of the early performance, and after it she rested in her dressing-room as usual. The cast rarely left the theatre between the two Saturday performances. There

226

was time for a meal in one's dressing-room, a brief rest, or a chat with the other actors, but no more. Grace had a standing order with the Trattoria for a tray to be sent over, and for this Philip usually joined her. Neither of them liked Saturday, but at least they had Sunday to look forward to — a whole day together with few demands from either of their careers. With luck, no demands at all.

And to-morrow was Sunday — a whole week since Maxine's unwelcome invasion of their private life. To Grace, it seemed longer. It seemed as if the girl's knowledge had hung like a shadow over their lives for a very long time indeed.

Tom Langley went over to the Trattoria for Grace's tray that evening. He carried it in with paternal care, anxious that she should have a good meal. "Make her eat every bite," he said to Philip in his fatherly way, and as usual Philip was touched by the old man's concern for his wife. Ever since they had befriended him Tom had been her devoted slave. Fetching trays and running errands for her were not part of his duties as stage director, but there was nothing Tom wouldn't do for her. He was like a shaggy old watch-dog, hovering over her protectively, and her watch-dog he would remain for the rest of his life.

To-day the old man lingered.

"Did Doctor Radcliffe bring news of Maxine?" he asked.

"Doctor Radcliffe?" Grace echoed in surprise. "Is he here?"

"He's been here for most of the performance. I thought he must have been waiting to speak to you."

"No — no, he didn't speak to me." Grace looked puzzled.

"That's odd," said Philip.

It was more than odd, thought Tom. There was no reason for David Radcliffe to come back-stage at the Comet when rehearsals for his play were not in progress. Even more odd was his reaction when Tom had found him climbing up and down the spiral staircase, examining the iron steps and searching the floor around the base. When he saw Tom, he had tried to pass the whole thing off.

"I wondered whether there was anything lying around belonging to my wife."

"What sort of thing?" Tom had asked.

"She might have dropped something. Her handbag might have fallen open."

But Philip Dunster had picked that up. He had held on to it until the ambulance came, and it had been fastened all the time, Tom remembered. He also remembered that Philip had made no reference to it, and that when Susan Howard asked for it the man pretended that it was his wife's. Tom had known that it was pretence, because Philip Dunster was no actor. He had tried to walk off with Maxine Culver's handbag for a very definite purpose, just as he must have been in the theatre for a very definite purpose.

And only yesterday he had telephoned the girl.

The more Tom thought about it the more suspicious it seemed and the more worried he became. He couldn't believe that a man like Philip had been carrying on with a girl like Maxine Culver, but one never knew. Everyone had their secrets, as he himself had, but the thought of an infidelity on Philip's part distressed him because of the pain it could cause Grace.

All day, Tom had been unable to get the matter out of his mind. All day, he had remembered the girl's spread-eagled body, and all day he had puzzled over Philip Dunster's presence in the theatre. His excuse about calling for Grace's bag was a thin one, and his pretence that the one he held was hers was equally unconvincing.

In fact, the whole incident was disturbing. There was something going on that he, Tom, didn't know about, and it had been going on ever since Maxine appeared for an audition and, later, was in Grace's dressing-room. Tom remembered walking in and finding her there, and he also remembered Grace declaring passionately, '*I could kill you for this!*'

And after that Maxine had got the part. In the face of all opposition Grace had insisted on her having it, and the reason was obvious. Maxine had blackmailed her into it.

Had she threatened to reveal that she was having an affair with Grace's husband and to blow the myth of their happy marriage wide open? It didn't seem possible, but Tom had lived long enough to learn that anything in this life was possible.

And now Maxine lay on the brink of death, after meeting Philip in the empty theatre before anyone else was around. That the girl had met Philip, Tom was now convinced.

And on top of this David Radcliffe had come back from the hospital to the theatre at a time when he had no reason to be present. Moreover, he had been careful not to draw attention to himself, staying quietly in the wings, waiting and searching. But for what?

Grace said, "If David is still around, will you ask him to come here? Perhaps he has news."

"I have," said David at the door. "Don't go away, Tom. You can hear this, too. Maxine's fall wasn't an accident."

David's eyes were on Philip, but he heard Grace give a faint gasp and saw her husband's hand go quickly to her shoulder. He looked at the pair of them and thought he had never known a nicer couple and that he hated doing this to them, but since he would be a more obvious suspect than Philip he had to learn the truth before he found himself in trouble up to his neck.

"You — you mean someone pushed her down the spiral stairs?" Grace said in a horrified whisper.

"No. She tripped — her spike heel snapped in one of the steps. She must have been hurrying down — and someone must have been hurrying after her, because when she fell she rolled down the curve and then over the side of the central well, grabbing the edge of the stairs, and her pursuer, whoever it was, struck or stamped on her fingers to make sure that she crashed to the ground."

Philip Dunster said, "So that is why you examined her hands this morning."

"And why I came back this afternoon. I've searched the spiral staircase and found the tip of a stiletto heel still wedged in one of the holes . . . "

"Where about?" Tom asked quickly. "How far up the stairs?"

"Just about level with the second floor, but that doesn't mean that she was coming down from that floor. She could have been running down from higher

232

up. I've been up there, too. There are a number of empty dressing-rooms at the top where she could have arranged to meet anyone privately."

Philip said, "If you are jumping to the conclusion that it was I who came down the stairs behind her, you are wrong. If I had arranged to meet Maxine Culver, I could have met her in my wife's dressing-room."

"But you came to look for Grace's handbag, didn't you? Nevertheless, you picked up Maxine's. Where was it? On the floor? Why did you pick it up? Why did you want it? Why was everyone anxious to get hold of it? It contained nothing but a lot of untidiness, believe me . . . "

"So you've examined it?" Grace said, a shade too quickly.

"Of course."

Tom Langley cut in, "While you're busy suspecting Mr. Dunster, why not suspect me? The top dressing-rooms are reserved for the men, irrespective of their status, so that the lower dressing-rooms on the first and second floors can be given to the women. I have a room at the very top, and Stephen Hammond has one on the floor below. So why not suspect us?"

"Hammond wasn't at the theatre this morning. Nor were you, until after Maxine was found."

"You don't know that. Either of us might have been."

"And were you?" David smiled a little as he put the question. Tom was too open, too guileless to be suspect. "As for Stephen Hammond, I know for a fact that he didn't come near the place. His fan mail was stacked on the doorkeeper's desk waiting to be collected. I saw it when I telephoned for the ambulance. And we all know Stephen — the first thing he does on arrival at the theatre is to collect his precious fan mail. He told me once how important it was. But on Saturdays he collects it when he comes for the first performance at five-thirty. As for you, the stage-doorkeeper tells me that he saw you only once — when you were leaving with Susan."

"I could have been here before. The man doesn't come on duty until eleven on Saturdays."

"And were you?" David repeated.

The old man turned away, saying nothing, and David continued, "You've all got to understand why I am asking these questions. It is important to me to find out who tried to kill Maxine, not only because her attacker shouldn't be allowed to get away with it, but because I am the one likely to be suspected — "

He broke off. He was facing the open door, and now the sound of a heavy footfall on the spiral staircase caught his attention. It was a slow, heavy tread, and he saw to his surprise that it belonged to Ethel Fothergill.

He had forgotten about Maxine's aunt. Now he watched her bulky figure descend, her middle-aged weight landing heavily on each tread. Coming downstairs like that, her step was as heavy as a man's.

He had forgotten something else, too — that Ethel's dressing-room was on the second floor.

18

WITH Della away for the day, time stretched ahead like a vacuum which Susan felt strangely disinclined to fill. There were several things she could do. Study her lines; iron her smalls; write to her parents; bake a cake, which neither she nor Della might eat, but which the importunate Spike McGee would certainly dispose of. But Spike managed to get enough for free as it was, a fact which some found amusing but which always outraged Susan's respectable upbringing.

"If you can't afford a thing, do without it," her parents always preached. "That way, you're beholden to no one."

But Spike didn't feel beholden to anyone in any way. Not even to Della, whom he made use of without conscience. "I give her a good time," he had said once. "She enjoys my company, so if I can't pay for it, why shouldn't she?" — all of which amused Della as much

236

as it disgusted Susan.

"When I've toppled Sean Connery from his perch," Spike would declare airily, "you'll be proud to have known me." But what little ambition he had and the negligible amount of energy he expended in pursuit of it wouldn't topple even a sparrow from its perch, thought Susan, and the sooner Della got him off her back the better.

"But I like him! He's fun. Besides, it makes no difference to him that I live in cheap rooms in a side street, which is more than can be said about *some* drama students!"

It was useless to point out that the luxury Della could go back to in Lowndes Square was common knowledge, and that Spike's apparently innocuous glance might well be focused on it. Della trusted everyone.

Susan tied her nearly-dry hair into a pony tail and departed for some street stalls off the Vauxhall Road where fruit and veg were sold at knock-down prices late on Saturday afternoon. She bought Bramleys, oranges, thin-skinned grapefruit, green peppers, and some aubergines which the local inhabitants had viewed with suspicion. The stall-holder was glad to get rid of experimental stock. She returned home planning the salad she would make for supper and the stuffing she would prepare for the peppers. Outside a delicatessen she counted her change and then went inside for pickled walnuts and a creamed Continental cheese to chop up with the grapefruit and add to the salad. Her fancy roamed. One day she would have a beautiful dining-table, shining mahogany reflecting the gleam of silver and crystal. Candlelight would flicker and the meal would be superlative — cooked by herself, of course — and across the table a man would say, "This is wonderful. *You* are wonderful . . . "

It was a romantic dream and one she indulged frequently. Hitherto the man had been a nebulous figure whom she vaguely knew to be the ideal man who would one day come along, but to-day he suddenly took form and shape and she realised with a sense of shock that it was David.

She thrust the dream aside. David was

married. He had a wife. That wife might be lying critically injured in St. Bede's Hospital, but it didn't mean that she was going to die, no matter how hopeless her case seemed. Miracles did happen and human beings sometimes survived the most appalling injury. The fact that she had to remind herself of these facts frightened Susan, for the implication was obvious. More than anything in the world she wished that David were free.

Now she was angry with herself. "Enough of that nonsense, my girl." That was what her father would say. As for her mother, with her sweet, practical, maternal concern she would warn her daughter never to fall in love with a married man. "There's no sense to it, love."

Nor was there, but the deed was done.

She wanted to run away from the thought, and even speeded her steps, her flat-heeled pumps hurrying along the street as if to aid her escape. But there was no escape from the truth and even to deny it was another form of retreat. Her footsteps slowed to a walking pace again and suddenly she realised that she was skirting the wall of St. Bede's and that ahead was the entrance to the casualty department. There was the very window where she had first seen David all that time ago. Suddenly she wanted to laugh. It was barely a week! A week to-morrow, to be exact. Midnight, as Big Ben tolled the hour and Monday, her big day, was ushered in.

As she crossed the road she wondered what time David went on duty and if she was likely to see him again before he did so. He had said nothing about another meeting. She wondered where he was right now and what he was doing. She had a fleeting impulse to call at the hospital to enquire about Maxine, and then her natural honesty prevented her. It would be no more than a gambit to see if David was around.

So she walked deliberately towards her own front door, and as she entered the narrow hall her landlady, talking into the telephone at the end of the passage, said, "Hold on a minute! She's here . . . "

Della's voice sounded far away.

"We're stuck at Sonning! That blasted

car Spike scrounged from his garage friend, what *do* you think, it was stolen! So here we are, at the local police station. Yes, honey, they actually pulled us in, bang in the middle of the village, just like that! Of course, Spike didn't know it was hot, how could he? He has just finished explaining to them and a perfectly sweet police sergeant let me use the phone. Well, actually there's a call box at the entrance, but he insisted on putting the coins in for me. They're dreamboats, all of them — the police, I mean — and I'll never call them names again even if they deserve it. They're going to let us go, but not with the car. Don't be silly, Sue, why should I come straight home? It would take *ages*. That's why I'm ringing — I thought you'd be worried when I didn't turn up to-night. We're going to scrounge a bed at that pub Spike's friends keep. Of *course*, two beds, stupid! Yes, of *course*, two rooms! Susan dear, do just listen to what I'm saying! I'll be home to-morrow morning. Did you get the latch-key all right? Spike was livid because I think he felt his nose put out of joint, but it did him good. What do you mean, *what* did him good? Being jealous, of course, but naturally I wasn't going to pass up an opportunity like that. He's been bad-tempered about it ever since and somehow I think it might be the end of a beautiful friendship . . . Don't inter*rupt*, Sue — time's running out. I'll tell you all about it to-morrow . . . "

The line cut off abruptly. Susan listened to the hollow echo of empty space, then replaced the receiver and went upstairs. She didn't know what on earth Della was nattering about, but if something had happened to make the parasitical Spike shy off, it was all to the good.

The flat seemed more empty than before and the vacuum of time even bigger. She felt disinclined to prepare a meal to eat alone, but she set about it diligently, determined to keep thought at bay. Busy hands meant a busy mind, or so she had always believed, but now she found that hers was busy in the wrong way. Stuffing green peppers didn't prevent her from thinking about David.

The dream took over again. She even

set the little card table which she and Della used for meals, placing two candles in the middle, two table mats, two sets of knives and forks, two side plates, two table napkins. She laughed at herself a little, remembering herself in childhood, playing at being mother. Sometimes she had set the table as a surprise for her own mother, buttercups in a jar, knives and forks the wrong way round, but always her mother had said, "That's beautiful, darling, really beautiful!"

The salad was an emerald island set in a bowl, and the red and yellow of tomato and grapefruit, the purple of the aubergines, the black walnuts, the white dices of cream cheese, were tropical plants splashing it with colour. Fruit in a cheap wooden bowl gleamed in the candlelight. ('That's wonderful,' said David. '*You* are wonderful . . . ').

Suddenly her cheeks were wet and she brushed them impatiently with the back of her hand, taking herself to task for being a fool. She would eat her meal and then go to see a film. She wouldn't let her heart take over.

The door-bell rang.

It was David.

"May I come in?" he said.

★ ★ ★

He didn't even notice the table. He looked strained and tired, unaware of his surroundings.

"I've just come from the hospital. Maxine is no better, no worse. I went straight there from the Comet."

"What were you doing at the Comet?"

"Hoping to learn things. I did learn some. The chief one was that I was right in suspecting that Maxine's fall wasn't wholly accidental."

He told her all he knew. They sat by the window and Big Ben boomed eight times from his tower. "I've an hour to spare before I go on duty," David said. "Is Della not back?"

"She's not coming. Have you eaten? There's enough for two, if you like to share it."

The stuffed peppers were good, the salad delicious. "That was wonderful," said David, when they had finished, but he didn't complete the rest of her dream sentence. All he did was to touch her cheek lightly when he left. "That's in thanks, Susan. Thanks for everything. More than all, thanks for being you."

Long after he had gone she sat by the window, looking out over London, hearing Big Ben boom the hours away. Once she thought she saw David's white-coated figure pass the Casualty window, but wasn't sure. Anyway, he didn't look up. But she didn't mind. She was happy. She had no real cause to be, but happy she was, and even the knowledge that back-stage this morning someone had lurked in the shadows, waiting for her to go, didn't mar her underlying sense of well-being. Even the awareness that if Maxine died David would be in an uneasy position didn't disturb her deeply, because she didn't really believe that it could happen, nor that anyone could doubt him. He was too honest, too open, too frank. She was convinced that the real person would be found and the guilt focused where it belonged.

But who *was* the real person? Philip Dunster? Tom Langley?

Her mind ran over everything that

David had said during supper.

"Let's count up the people who were at the theatre this morning. Dunster, Tom Langley, you and me. Tom Langley didn't arrive until after we did, and we didn't arrive until after Maxine had crashed down the spiral stairs. Dunster claims that he didn't, either. But none of us can be vouched for."

"I can vouch for you. I met you coming in."

"I might have been there earlier, gone away, and come back again. *I* might have lurked in the shadows when you first arrived."

"But you didn't."

"No, I didn't. Langley might have done. Dunster, too. But what motive would either of them have? If it comes to that, no one seems to have a motive except me and — "

He had broken off at that point.

"Were you going to say that I had? Everyone knows that I would have been glad to see Maxine lose the part — the part I had set my heart on."

"In a person like you, that wouldn't be a sufficient motive for violence."

"But you don't know me."

"In a short time I've come a long way towards doing so. Besides, doctors are pretty adept at summing people up, apart from which I've been studying psychology since I got my M.B. I hope to specialise in psychiatrics."

She went to bed thinking about David, wondering who he had meant in that odd, cryptic sentence, if not herself.

It was midnight when she left her window seat. If she had waited a minute longer she would have seen Tom Langley walk along the street and turn into the casualty department of St. Bede's.

19

IT was a quiet night despite the fact that it was Saturday. Drunks, street accidents, the occasional attempted suicide and the usual run of injuries were the general Saturday-night quota in the casualty ward, but by midnight the worst was over and David paused for a cup of coffee.

Casualty sister looked at him sympathetically, but he avoided her glance. The reports about Maxine which had been telephoned down to him from time to time plainly interested the woman and he was well aware that his wife's admittance had been a topic of conversation amongst the hospital staff. He could sense it in the abrupt silences which recurred whenever he appeared, in the sympathetic glances, in the general anxiety to make things easy for him. Two doctors had even offered to take over his casualty duty, but he was thankful to be back at work.

Now he accepted the coffee gratefully

and was settling down to drink it — without any probing conversation from sister, he hoped — when a nurse came in search of him.

"There's a gentleman asking for you, Doctor. Not a patient. He says it's personal."

The last person David expected to see was the elderly actor. In the clinical hall he looked a picturesque figure with his sweeping hat-brim, and overcoat, as always, cloak-wise over his shoulders. David almost expected to see a hansom cab waiting outside.

"I must talk to you," Tom said. His voice was as tired as his smile, but there was an air of resolution about him. "I've something to tell you."

The hall porter was sitting in his cubby-hole reading a paper. A nurse was wheeling a dressing trolley towards them. Casualty sister could pass by at any moment. Everyone was occupied, but snatches of conversation could be overheard.

"Come in here," said David, leading Tom into an examination room. It was one of a series of cubicles with open tops

249

and lightwood screens, but at least it was private.

"What do you want to tell me?" David said in a lowered voice.

"Simply this. I did it. I was with Maxine at the theatre this morning. I was the one who tried to kill her."

★ ★ ★

David looked at the old man for a long moment, then said, "I don't believe you."

"It's true. She was blackmailing me, threatening me — "

"With what?"

"With the truth about my past. I once did something foolish, and she knew about it. She threatened to tell everyone, particularly the management — "

"That means Grace."

"Not entirely. Philip Dunster is the backer and has a large say in things."

"But they are your friends!"

"They've been good to me, yes. Philip Dunster I hardly know, but Grace I've known for a long time. It is thanks to her that I got on my feet again."

"Then this thing — whatever it was you did — she already knows about?"

"No. We'd lost touch completely, then she heard of my wife's death, and because Sylvia — that was my wife — had once been kind to her, Grace went out of her way to find me. She'd been playing on Broadway for a long season, then filming in Hollywood, so by the time she came back to England and heard of Sylvia's death many months had passed and I had gone to earth in a cheap room in Brixton. I never went near the old theatrical haunts because I couldn't afford them. I was finding it impossible to get a job. I had stolen some money, you see — "

David said gently, "You don't have to tell me about it. It must have happened a long time ago and you suffered for it. We don't all go around doing the right thing all the time, you know."

Tom's guileless old eyes dimmed.

"You're a very understanding young man, Doctor Radcliffe."

"No. I'm a human being, like yourself."

"You ought to hate me for what I tried to do to your wife."

"I could hardly hate someone who, in

251

a moment of panic, went berserk."

"That was it — " Tom said tremulously. "A moment of panic. When Grace came back into my life she thought I was merely down on my luck, going through a bad patch the way actors sometimes do. I had given up trying to be an actor because I knew I would never be a star, and turned to road management instead. When this thing happened we were on tour, and Sylvia was taken ill. Desperately ill. That was a moment of panic, too . . . "

"So you wanted her to have the best, you wanted to save her, and there wasn't any National Health Service in those days. Specialists cost money, and you had to have it." David's hand fell upon the old man's shoulder. "Stop condemning yourself. It is all in the past."

"So I thought, until Maxine turned up. She was on that tour too, and to my horror she remembered about it. She reminded me of it very subtly on the morning of the first rehearsal. I was upstairs in the dressing-room I use as a sort of office, and I heard someone coming up — a woman. It struck me as odd because the footsteps came nearer and nearer, so I knew that she, whoever she was, was visiting one of the men's dressing-rooms . . . "

"Yours? Had she come to see you?"

"No. Stephen Hammond. I couldn't think why, until he arrived. All she wanted was his autograph, and to make sure of getting him alone she waited for him in his dressing-room. I heard her tell him so, because I'd come out of my room to listen. I was standing at the top of the spiral staircase, thinking that I could hear the woman moving about in his room . . . "

"Moving about? In what way?"

"It sounded to me as if she were searching it, but suddenly everything was quiet so I didn't go downstairs to check up, and anyway Stephen arrived and I heard her telling him why she was there. It was all perfectly harmless, but of course I shouldn't have listened. I should have gone back to my room, and I was just about to when she came out of Stephen's. She must have heard me, because she looked up and smiled and said in a significant sort of way how glad she was that I had got on my feet again. I knew what she meant — that she remembered about my past and that I would be wise to realise it."

"And that began it — her threats, I mean."

"Yes. I think she enjoyed a sense of power over people. I'm sorry. I know she's your wife, but I don't like her. Then on Friday she said she wanted to talk to me and that she would come to the theatre before the understudy rehearsal next morning, between ten and half past, and I had no choice but to agree. I told her I'd wait upstairs in my room."

"And when you met there, what did she say?"

"That if I didn't use my influence to stop Stephen Hammond from trying to get rid of her, she would tell Grace about my being sacked, and why. I couldn't bear the thought of Grace knowing about it. Besides, my job at the Comet is my life. I love it. I'm happy there."

The sensitive, veined hands were trembling. David said gently, "Do you really think it would have made a difference to Grace? She's a warm, human person, and she's deeply fond of you."

"You don't understand. *I just didn't want her to know*. I couldn't bear the thought of it. And even if it didn't make any difference to Grace, I wasn't so sure about Dunster. I've always had the feeling that he tolerated me for his wife's sake, the way he tolerates other people in the theatrical profession, but how he would feel if he knew that their trusted stage director had been sacked for theft, was another matter."

"And so you panicked."

"Yes. I couldn't hide it from Maxine, either, and she laughed in my face. She was still laughing when she went down the stairs. She was approaching the second floor when she tripped and went pitching downwards. I ran after her at once and had just caught up with her when she dropped over the middle of the spiral, made a grab at the side of the steps, and clung there. And then — I did it. I couldn't stop myself."

"And what happened then?"

Tom's head jerked up with an air of surprise.

"It's obvious, surely? I left the theatre and came back later, carrying a flask of coffee from the Trattoria as if I'd just arrived."

"But before you left the theatre you hid, didn't you? Just for a few minutes because someone came. Maybe you didn't see who it was, but it was Susan. She thought she heard a door shut very softly. Was that you?"

The old man nodded.

"Where did you hide?"

"Well, there's only one room leading from the wings, except the prop room and that's on the opposite side."

"You mean Grace Challoner's dressing-room?"

"Of course."

"So you hid in there. And if Philip Dunster had been there, you would have seen him, wouldn't you? So that puts him in the clear, doesn't it?"

"Yes."

"So it seems that his story about arriving later to collect his wife's handbag was true . . . "

"Yes." There seemed only one thing more to say, and Tom said it. "What are you going to do now?"

"Precisely nothing," said David.

"*Nothing*? But I've confessed!"

"So all right, you've confessed. You've got it off your chest. Now go home and get a good night's sleep."

Tom rose shakily. "But I — I don't understand — "

David smiled. "Go home, there's a good chap. I've got work to do, and from the sound of things I'd say a patient was being wheeled into Casualty right at this moment."

He watched the old man walk away down the corridor, coat swinging, shoulders bent. He looked very tired. As well he might be, thought David. He had just put up the best performance of his life.

20

IT seemed to Grace Challoner that Sunday was a breathless hiatus in which time stood still, a prolonged interval before the curtain finally rose on a climax which would either save them or break them. Philip sensed her tension and was aware of her effort to hide it, but there was little he could do to ease her mind until the morning.

"I will go to Australia House first thing," he promised yet again. "Their files of the *Sydney Morning Herald* go back years. I'll search until I find that damned report, and if that doesn't yield all the information we want I'll get it through the Home Office, or Scotland Yard, or any channel necessary, but *I'll get it, understand*? And whatever the outcome nothing will ever make me stop loving you and nothing will ever make me think of you as anything but my wife. If by some awful mischance Lew Martin is still alive, you have ample grounds for divorce. Criminal grounds."

"And the whole story will become public property, you know that, don't you? Not only the fact that you've married a bigamist will be splashed across the front page of every newspaper in the country, but the fact that I featured in his trial, too."

"Then we'll just have to face it together. In any case, a bigamist is a person who marries another while knowing full well that their first partner is not only still alive, but still married to them. You believed him dead, with just cause. I don't call that bigamy."

"Others will. It will make malicious tongues wag."

"Malicious tongues always wag."

"These could be damaging — for you."

He silenced her with a kiss.

They were sitting in the paved garden at the rear of their Westminster house, having mid-morning coffee. The peace of London on a Sunday surrounded them. It seemed hard to believe that beyond the garden wall trouble and scandal and fear just waited to pounce. For the moment all was shut out; they were enclosed in their own private world, and Grace knew that so long as everything was right in that world fear was illogical. Nevertheless, it had stalked like a ghost ever since David Radcliffe had come to her dressing-room and announced that someone had attempted to kill his wife.

And because Philip had gone to the theatre to meet her, he would be the obvious suspect. The thought lay between them now, unacknowledged, unspoken. If Maxine did die, and if an enquiry followed, it would be impossible to cling long to that tale about the handbag. It was too thin to be convincing.

But Philip's nearness was a comfort to her, his solidity a reassuring bulwark. She snuggled against him and the garden hammock swung a little as she moved. Philip put his arm about her and they just sat there, swinging gently in the hammock, waiting for time to pass, treasuring these moments together, loving each other as they had loved almost from their first moment of meeting.

Grace thought frantically, Nothing can

break up a marriage like ours, and it *is* a marriage, a real marriage, no matter what laws or conventions might say!

As if sensing her thoughts, Philip said, "You know, don't you, that whatever happens nothing can come between us?"

She didn't have time to answer, because at that moment the sharp peal of the front door-bell echoed imperatively through the house. Philip uttered an impatient sound. It wasn't unusual for some political issue to interfere with their Sunday privacy, but to-day, more than any other, it was far from welcome.

Later, Grace thought it strange that neither of them should associate that urgent summons with the crisis at the theatre, but Sunday was respected in the theatrical world as the one day in the week when a star could be left alone; in politics it was different, so Philip heaved a great sigh, dragged himself up from the hammock, and went to answer the door himself.

Grace remained where she was, hoping that Philip was not to be whisked away from her even for an hour, and then turned her head and saw young Doctor Radcliffe coming towards her from the house.

"David has news," Philip said. "Tom Langley has confessed to attacking Maxine."

Grace sat up, her face shocked.

"I don't believe it!"

"It's true," David told her. "He came to the hospital last night, and told me the whole story. She had been threatening him with exposure."

"What sort of exposure?"

"About his past. He made a mistake, long ago, and she knew about it. She threatened to tell you."

Grace gave a sort of incredulous laugh that finished in a sob.

"Not *that* awful business, all those years ago! But I've always known about that! I heard about it in a roundabout way when I returned to England from Hollywood and I promptly set about finding him. Poor, darling old Tom! Did he really think I didn't know?"

"He quite genuinely thought so. I told him I felt sure it would make no difference to you."

"He should know that without being told!"

"The very possibility of your knowing distressed him. He couldn't bear the thought of it."

"I can believe that," said Philip. "He is devoted to my wife. You never told me what his secret was, Grace, but I knew there was something — your anxiety to help him pointed to that. But this business about his attacking Maxine — do you believe it, Radcliffe?"

"No," David answered bluntly. "I think he was lying to protect you."

There was a brief silence. Beyond the high garden wall the sound of a distant river steamer echoed from the Thames. A bee droned amongst the tubs of flowers. The garden hammock creaked, swinging back violently as Grace jumped up.

"You don't believe that!" she cried.

"That he was trying to protect your husband? Yes, I do."

"I meant that it was *necessary* to protect him!"

"That, I don't know."

"Well, *I* do — "

Philip interrupted quietly, "I think we

263

should tell David everything, Grace."

"I hope you will. That's why I'm here. When I left the hospital a quarter of an hour ago the bulletin on Maxine was serious. She has a few more hours to live, if that."

Philip said nothing, merely indicating a garden chair and urging his wife into the hammock again. He sat down beside her. Their fingers linked.

"It began," said Philip, "when your wife called on Ethel Fothergill last Sunday night . . ."

It didn't take long to tell. The whole thing, from the time that Maxine flaunted the newspaper cutting in Grace's face to the time that Philip telephoned her at the theatre and suggested a meeting the next morning, was related in a matter of minutes. David listened impassively, but the story of his wife's unscrupulous bargaining horrified him.

"I knew she would come to meet me," Philip said, "because I made it plain on the phone that although she could intimidate poor Grace, she couldn't intimidate me. I told her to bring the remainder of the newspaper cutting and implied that I wouldn't be averse to buying it if necessary, although I actually had no intention of being so weak. That was merely bait, to make sure that she turned up, but I was surprised to find that she had arrived before me. I expected that being late would be part of her act — to pretend that she had the upper hand and to make me appear too anxious. I arrived dead on time, went to Grace's dressing-room, and waited. I must have been there for no more than a couple of minutes when I glanced through the open door towards the stage — and saw her lying there. You know the result. I picked up her handbag, and then went to telephone for help. I couldn't get an outside line — then you arrived, with Susan Howard. I wanted the handbag, because I knew the cutting would be in it."

He broke off. David was staring in sudden recollection.

"That newspaper cutting! *I* have it! I pushed it aside because it meant nothing to me. I thought it must refer to someone she knew, people I had never heard of." He was rummaging through his pockets.

"I wore this suit yesterday. I shoved the bit of newspaper away, scarcely glancing at it. The names didn't register, you see. Nothing about its registered . . . "

"Not even *my* name?" Grace asked. "Maxine told me it was mentioned."

"All I remember is something about escaped prisoners. Three, I believe. Here . . . "

The cutting was short, dog-eared, and said very little. Grace read it over her husband's shoulder and when she was through she began to laugh. Her laughter rose on a hysterical note, and he shook her hard.

"Stop it," he commanded. "Stop it, darling."

The sound switched off abruptly and she subsided against him, crying with relief.

"May I read it again?" David asked, and Philip handed it across without a word.

All it said was that three men named Carl Jonsen, Pete Riddle and Red Clayburn had escaped from Long Bay Jail, Sydney, on the night of June 13 and had been caught when trying to stow away on a vessel in the harbour. "Two of the men are pictured above at the wedding of the notorious Luigi Martinelli, alias Lew Martin, with whom they received prolonged sentences for crimes ranging from robbery with violence to drug peddling. This is the third attempt at jail-breaking made by Jonsen and Riddle since conviction. Martinelli died in prison two years after being sentenced."

"The photograph showed Martinelli's bride," Philip told David, "Grace, at the age of seventeen. It also showed another woman, who was a guest at the wedding — Maxine's aunt, Ethel Fothergill. Maxine recognised both, and hit on the diabolical idea of tearing the report in half and blackmailing Grace with the belief that her husband was not only still alive, but on the run. Taken out of context there was nothing to prove that he wasn't. The headline said three men had escaped — and the photograph showed the only three that Grace had heard about. Maxine cut the photograph out, plus headline, and kept the rest back as an additional threat, implying that Martinelli was the third man. All the time, of course, she knew that he was dead. But she wasn't so clever as she thought — and she didn't know me. I had every intention of digging up the truth, no matter what it was."

"So poor Tom Langley has lied for nothing," said Grace.

"If he has lied," Philip answered. "He would do anything to protect you, anything at all, I'm sure of that. And don't forget that he came on the scene when Maxine was in your dressing-room. He heard what you said to her. You told me about it — remember?"

"That I could kill her — that's what I said. 'I could kill you for this,' I told her, and the door opened and Tom walked in. Yes — he heard me, but he surely couldn't think that I meant it!"

"Do we ever really know what another person thinks?" Philip replied. "The only way to find out now is to go to see him. We'll tell him everything, and then persuade *him* to tell *us*."

They were walking across the garden towards the house when David said quietly, "But don't forget that although we are convinced that Tom is lying, and although we know that none of us was responsible, *someone* must have been, because someone did make sure that Maxine fell to her death."

"Which means someone else whose security she threatened," Philip added.

Grace stopped dead in her tracks.

"If you mean Ethel, I don't believe it."

"She was the only other person who was likely to suffer if Maxine succeeded in making trouble. If scandal did undermine the Comet Theatre Company then her security would be undermined, too."

"But once Maxine got the part, Ethel believed there was no danger of that."

"Then the only alternative seems to be Tom. Perhaps he wasn't lying to protect us, or you. Perhaps the story he gave David was true."

"I still don't believe it. There *must* be another alternative yet, another person . . . "

"I think there is," David put in, "but I can't prove it. I haven't a shred of evidence. It's all conjecture based on one disturbing fact — that he's too blatantly innocent — that he couldn't possibly have done it because he wasn't anywhere near, that no one saw him, that his mail was untouched, a thing he is virtually incapable of resisting . . . "

"*Stephen?*"

"Who else?"

"But why? *Why?*"

"I think I know why," David answered with pity in his voice.

After he left, he went straight back to the hospital. It seemed strange to walk through the familiar doors not as a doctor, but as the relative of a patient on the critical list.

Half an hour after his return, Maxine died.

21

DELLA arrived back shortly before midday with one and sixpence, an enormous appetite, and no Spike McGee.

"I only had enough for my own train ticket, and he was livid, which seemed a bit unfair, I must say. His pub friends gave us house room, but no more — not even breakfast. I had a sort of feeling that we weren't welcome, which struck me as odd since Spike had said they were the friends of his bosom."

"Perhaps he wasn't one of theirs," Susan answered dryly. "Perhaps they've given him so much house room in the past that they're disenchanted with him — which I hope *you* will be, after this."

"Poor old Spike," Della mumbled as she downed three rashers of bacon, two eggs, four slices of toast and three cups of coffee. "He had to hitch-hike back, so I suppose he's still on the road somewhere."

"If I know Spike, he'll not only scrounge a lift but a lunch, as well. You don't need to worry about him — he's the champion parasite of all London."

"You sound as if you don't like him," Della said in mock surprise.

"However did you guess?"

Della heaved a sigh of satisfaction. "Goodness, but I feel better for this!"

She clasped her hands round the cup and surveyed the room affectionately. "You've been doing things. Spring cleaning or something. Is that how you spent a lonely week-end?"

"On my bendeds," Susan acknowledged with an air of martyrdom.

"If I had more than one and sixpence until Monday, I'd take you to a film to make up for it. Did you really spend all your time doing chores?"

"I also washed my hair and my smalls."

"Stop it, you're making me cry."

Susan laughed. It sounded like a deadly week-end, but actually it had been one of the most eventful she had ever known. She felt oddly reluctant to tell Della about Maxine's accident; reluctant even to think about David's wife. Besides, there was plenty of time to get around to that. A long, quiet Sunday stretched ahead, barren because it held no specific promise of seeing David again.

Della began to wash up, tipping soap powder recklessly into the water. "You'll never learn," sighed Susan. "I'll have to ration that stuff. Make sure you marry a man rich enough to keep you in detergents."

"Would a policeman's pay be enough, d'you think?" Della mused romantically.

"A *policeman*? Don't tell me you fell for the one you told me about on the phone last night?"

"Well, he was rather fab. It's a pity he's going on night duty as from to-day. The wonderful thing was that he thought I was just a misguided working girl in need of care and protection. It was a nice feeling, especially after Spike had suggested I should put a reverse-charge call through to my parents and ask for a car to be sent to bring us back to town. 'They've got a fleet,' he said,

273

'surely they can spare one to rescue a stranded daughter?'"

"Plus her stranded escort, of course."

"Well, he didn't actually *say* it . . . But what cut me to the quick was finding out that he knew so much about them."

"I rather suspected he did," Susan said gently.

"Of course, he was feeling a bit rattled before we even reached Sonning. We quarrelled the whole way there. And then to be picked up by the police and accused of stealing a car — "

"Very trying," Susan agreed. "My heart bleeds for him."

"Well, it *was* trying until he proved his innocence. They let him go because he gave them the name and address of his garage friend and offered to identify him in court if necessary."

"Charming. He'd send his own mother up the river, that one. If you've quarrelled with him for good, I'm thankful. What was it all about, anyway? Big enough to last for ever, I hope."

Della dried her hands, smiling in amused recollection.

"Actually, it was the silliest thing. I'll

show you. It's in the pocket of my duffel . . . "

Her blue-jeaned legs skipped towards her room. A moment later she returned, bearing a scrap of paper.

"It was all over *this*, would you believe it? Why Spike had to take on so, I just don't know, because actually he's awfully disappointing off-stage, isn't he? So much older than I thought. Honestly, it was ridiculous of Spike to be jealous — " Della broke off. "What's the matter?"

Susan was staring at the scrap of paper. It was a piece torn from a pocket book and exactly matched that on which Della had scribbled the note accompanying the latch-key.

"Where — *when* — did you get that?" she whispered.

Della answered in bewilderment, "Yesterday. When we came back with your latch-key. I hadn't any paper so I made Spike tear a piece out of his precious pocket-book. The doorkeeper wasn't there and so I wrapped the note round your key and pushed it in the H pigeon-hole — "

"No — this, *this*!" Susan demanded

impatiently. "*When did you get this?*"

"At the same time, of course. He came out of the theatre right at that moment and I couldn't let a chance like that pass by. And he was sweet about it, even though he was in a tearing hurry. I thought you said he wouldn't be at the theatre on Saturday morning . . . Sue, what *is* the matter?"

"Go on, go *on!*"

"With what? There isn't any more. I grabbed Spike's pocket book and asked for an autograph and he gave it to me and flashed a smile and hurried away, and Spike was stupid to be jealous just because he wrote a personal message. Actually, I thought it rather silly, '*With love to a pretty fan* . . . ' I ask you! But I suppose he scribbles that sort of thing automatically. I must say, he struck me as rather conceited and not a bit handsome. In fact, he was looking awful. Sort of wild-eye and agitated. You should have seen his hands shaking — Well, just look at his writing! I felt sure he was ill. Susan, for goodness' sake, why are you looking like that?"

Susan didn't answer. She simply grabbed

Della by the hand and rushed her out of the flat. As they ran downstairs she panted, "The time? What *time* was it, for heaven's sake?"

"Honey, how should I know? I didn't look at my watch, but it couldn't have been long after we left you because I found the key within a matter of minutes and made Spike turn round and come back. Because the doorkeeper wasn't there, I couldn't ask for you, and anyway I knew you'd gone down to the stage for rehearsals. Will you *please* tell me where we are going?"

Susan didn't bother. She rushed her friend across the street and into the hospital.

Doctor Radcliffe wasn't on duty. He had been into the hospital and gone away again.

"If you've come to enquire about his wife," the porter said, "I'm sorry to say she died this morning. Doctor Radcliffe went home shortly after it happened. He'll be excused duty for the rest of the day, I imagine."

It was Della who took over now. She led Susan out into the street and waited while the girl took a deep, steadying breath. She couldn't understand why the death of David Radcliffe's wife should upset her so. Wasn't she the girl who had grabbed the part of Nina, the girl everyone at the theatre disliked? Susan had given Della a day-to-day account of rehearsals, and of everyone connected with them, thus Della knew that young Doctor Radcliffe was not only the author of the play, but the angry young man who had stormed out of the flat after hurling the truth about his marriage at Susan's stunned head. In the circumstances, it would be hypocritical to pretend that Maxine's sudden death could cause anyone any grief.

"Come home," Della said gently. "I'll make you a good strong cup of coffee."

"I don't want it. I want to see David. I *must* see David . . . "

"Right now? And what's all this about his wife? I didn't even know she was ill."

"She wasn't. She had an accident yesterday morning. She fell down a spiral staircase. It happened in the theatre just before I arrived, but I didn't see her because the place was in darkness and no one was there. At least, I thought no one was there. So I went away for a cup of coffee, and that must have been when you came back — and Stephen Hammond followed me out." Susan was steadier now. "So that is why I must see David right away. It's terribly important, otherwise they might think that he . . . *he* . . . "

"All right," said Della, thrusting aside further questions, "we'll go to him right now. Where does he live?"

The extraordinary thing was that Susan didn't know. She shook her head numbly, thinking how stupid it was to love a man and not even know where he lived.

"He once told me he had a flat a few blocks away because it was close to the hospital — "

"Wait a minute."

The hall porter was surprised to see Blue-Jeans back. He smiled at her pert little face, thinking how pretty girls were nowadays and why people disapproved of them he couldn't understand. This one was certainly worth looking at, and so was her friend with the smoky-blue eyes.

He had noticed those eyes, almost too big for her pale little face.

Della said in a hushed voice, "I'd like to send a letter of condolence to Doctor Radcliffe. May I have his address?"

"Well now, miss, I'm not supposed to give addresses of the medical staff to callers. If you write to him here — "

"If I write to him here he won't get it until he comes back on duty, and in the circumstances he'll be given leave of absence, won't he? At a time like this it would be cruel to withhold the sympathy of his friends."

The reproach in her voice was more than a susceptible male could withstand.

Five minutes later David was opening his front door to them. Five minutes later Susan was thrusting the scrap of paper into his hand and stammering, "Della can prove it, she can identify him, he won't be able to deny it — it is *there*, all the proof we need . . . "

22

STEPHEN HAMMOND didn't attempt to deny it. He sat slumped in an arm-chair when David called on him — a near-wreck of a man too terrified of life to make any attempt to fight for it. David's professional glance took in the betraying pupils of the eyes, the hands, the ghastly pallor, all the horrible symptoms of the addict who needed help and sought it in only one way.

David pulled up a chair and sat down beside him and said, "I can help you, if you'll let me. You can be cured because it is not too late. When it is too late you will be a complete wreck, worse than any alcoholic, doomed to only a living death. I won't give you the horrifying details, but I can show them to you at a special clinic where doctors still strive to help cases already beyond it."

"I don't want help. Not now . . . not now . . . "

The voice was incoherent, mumbling, but David caught the words and said, "You mean because of what you did to Maxine?"

The hopeless eyes scanned David's face.

"She's dead, isn't she?"

"Yes."

Suddenly, Stephen buried his face in his hands. "I did it, *I did it*! But you know that and that's why you're here . . ."

"I'm here to help you."

"How? By handing me over to the police?"

David pushed him gently back into the chair.

"Tell me about it. All of it. Try to remember everything, because that will help when I make my report. A medical report, you understand. You'll be taken care of . . ."

"In prison?" Stephen asked hoarsely.

"In a hospital. You will be there for months, but when you come out you will be your normal self again. But understand this — I can only make sure that you go there if you tell me absolutely everything, right from the beginning . . . "

Stephen answered wearily, "Since you know so much, haven't you guessed the rest?"

"That Maxine recognised your weakness, yes. That she searched your dressing-room one morning and found what she was looking for. You didn't realise this until after she had gone because she made some excuse about wanting your autograph and kept you talking so that you wouldn't notice the forced lock on the drawer until she got away from your dressing-room. And then, of course, she knew that she had the upper hand — she could threaten you with her knowledge any time she chose, but meanwhile she preferred to keep you dangling, waiting on tenterhooks . . . "

"She played with me like a cat with a mouse," Stephen whispered. "She mocked me and tortured me, playing some sadistic game of her own. At first I tried to ignore her, then to get rid of her. I begged Grace to dismiss her, but she wouldn't. She even said she couldn't! Then on Friday, when I could stand it no longer and my nerves were getting raw and I was desperate for — for help — you know the kind I mean — "

"I know the kind you mean."

"I asked her to meet me early at the theatre. I knew the stage-doorkeeper didn't come on duty until eleven so I suggested ten-thirty. She insisted on ten o'clock. She had another appointment, she said, so ten it had to be."

"No one else was in the theatre when you arrived?"

"No."

"And no one came when you were there?"

Stephen shook a bewildered head.

"Not — not until later — just when I was about to escape . . . "

"That was when you hid in Grace's dressing-room?"

Stephen nodded mutely. "I — I didn't have any plan to hurt Maxine, you understand, but I — I wasn't myself . . . "

"I know."

"Well — she came. She said she was in a hurry and kept referring to this other appointment. She didn't say where and I wasn't interested, anyway. I just

284

begged her to give back the stuff she had taken from my dressing-room and she — she — "

"She laughed. She taunted you. She goaded you into a fury . . . "

"And then she gave it to me. She gave it to me with the sweetest smile and said she was sorry to have teased me and she hoped I hadn't really taken her seriously and for a moment she had me absolutely fooled. I stood there with the little package in my hand, sobbing like a bloody two-year-old, hating myself. Have you any idea how much a man in my state loathes himself?"

"If he does loathe himself, it is a good sign. That only happens in the early stage, the curable stage. Later, he doesn't care. Go on. What did Maxine do then?"

"She left me. I heard her going downstairs. I opened the package — the stuff was in an envelope — and there was nothing inside but sugar. Powdered sugar! The stuff used for icing cakes . . . " The ravaged face twisted in a bitter smile. "She'd hoodwinked me completely and I — I went berserk. I raced after her and suddenly she was frightened. I remember her looking back for a moment and her whole face changed. She was terrified. Then she ran — and fell. She rolled down the stairs, bumping violently from step to step, then pitched over the side, the side of the centre well, and clung there and I . . . I . . . I made sure that she fell . . . "

Suddenly Stephen crumpled like a puppet with broken strings. He was no longer recognisable as the dashing, debonair actor of stage and screen. All the bravado had gone out of him and his last uncertain hold on departing youth slipped out of his grasp.

And now he'll be all right, thought David with compassion. Now that he's stopped craving to be young he will learn to accept the passing of time, to be himself, to live normally.

"If you will come with me now," he said gently, "I promise you will be taken care of."

23

"WHAT will become of him?" Grace asked in distress.

"He will be charged with attempting to cause malicious bodily harm, and discharged on the grounds of diminished responsibility. He will then be given hospital treatment over a period of months, coupled with psychiatric treatment, and at the end of it he will emerge a different man. Healthy, normal, middle-aged, and not afraid of growing old. But you will have to find another leading man, because he will no longer be able to play the dashing young lover or the romantic lead. And believe it or not, he won't even mind. He will probably have just as successful a career playing character parts."

They were sitting in David's flat — Philip and Grace and Ethel, David and Susan and Della. Stephen lay in a hospital bed, no longer tortured and frightened and desperate. The Dunsters had insisted on seeing him when David telephoned to tell them the story, and later old Tom Langley had come too, then Ethel. They were Stephen's friends and so they rallied round, and when he came back to normal life again they would be there, waiting for him, still his friends, loyal as theatrical folk are always loyal to their colleagues.

Susan was very quiet. She had sat beside David ever since his return, saying nothing, but as aware of him as he was of her. Della sat cross-legged on the hearth-rug, awed by the famous company in which she found herself. She also felt rather important, because if she hadn't returned to the theatre at that precise moment and waylaid Stephen Hammond for his autograph and if vanity, poor man, hadn't been his Achilles heel, how would anyone have found out the truth? At any rate, not so soon. Not until red-tape and official enquiries and police investigation had got to work.

So she felt she had good reason to be proud, and had preened without embarrassment when David thanked her. When the others did too, she felt practically airborne.

Now she looked at Susan and then at David, and although neither was looking at the other she suddenly knew that they wanted to be alone.

"It's time we went," she announced abruptly, and the others agreed, but when Susan rose along with them Della said under her breath, "Not you, twit. I want to make a call to Sonning. The cheap rate is still on and I can have three minutes thanking a certain representative of the law for being kind to me yesterday. Think he'll like that?"

"It will certainly brighten his night duty," Susan assured her solemnly.

David saw his guests to the street door and stood for a while watching their departure. Philip and Grace drove off into the night; Tom and Ethel declined a lift and walked away down the street; Della skipped across the road, her bright head shining in the lamplight.

Slowly Big Ben chimed the hour, and Ethel Fothergill paused to listen.

"Midnight," she said. "It was this time last Sunday that it all began . . . "

Driving home with Philip, Grace was

289

saying the same thing. "It's impossible to believe that so much has happened in a week. It's like the end of a horrible dream."

Her husband took one hand from the wheel and squeezed hers affectionately, loving her as always, letting her know as always.

David listened to Big Ben too, then closed the door and went back upstairs. He was aware of a sense of glowing anticipation; more than all, of an abounding happiness because he was going upstairs to be alone with Nina, the girl of his dreams . . .

Except that her name was Susan.

THE END

TIGER TIGER
Frank Ryan

A young man involved in drugs is found murdered. This is the first event which will draw Detective Inspector Sandy Woodings into a whirlpool of murder and deceit.

CAROLINE MINUSCULE
Andrew Taylor

Caroline Minuscule, a medieval script, is the first clue to the whereabouts of a cache of diamonds. The search becomes a deadly kind of fairy story in which several murders have an other-worldly quality.

LONG CHAIN OF DEATH
Sarah Wolf

During the Second World War four American teenagers from the same town join the Army together. Forty-two years later, the son of one of the soldiers realises that someone is systematically wiping out the families of the four men.

CLOUD OVER MALVERTON
Nancy Buckingham

Dulcie soon realises that something is seriously wrong at Malverton, and when violence strikes she is horrified to find herself under suspicion of murder.

AFTER THOUGHTS
Max Bygraves

The Cockney entertainer tells stories of his East End childhood, of his RAF days, and his post-war showbusiness successes and friendships with fellow comedians.

MOONLIGHT AND MARCH ROSES
D. Y. Cameron

Lynn's search to trace a missing girl takes her to Spain, where she meets Clive Hendon. While untangling the situation, she untangles her emotions and decides on her own future.

THE WILDERNESS WALK
Sheila Bishop

Stifling unpleasant memories of a misbegotten romance in Cleave with Lord Francis Aubrey, Lavinia goes on holiday there with her sister. The two women are thrust into a romantic intrigue involving none other than Lord Francis.

THE RELUCTANT GUEST
Rosalind Brett

Ann Calvert went to spend a month on a South African farm with Theo Borland and his sister. They both proved to be different from her first idea of them, and there was Storr Peterson — the most disturbing man she had ever met.

ONE ENCHANTED SUMMER
Anne Tedlock Brooks

A tale of mystery and romance and a girl who found both during one enchanted summer.

BUTTERFLY MONTANE
Dorothy Cork

Parma had come to New Guinea to marry Alec Rivers, but she found him completely disinterested and that overbearing Pierce Adams getting entirely the wrong idea about her.

HONOURABLE FRIENDS
Janet Daley

Priscilla Burford is happily married when she meets Junior Environment Minister Alistair Thurston. Inevitably, sexual obsession and political necessity collide.

WANDERING MINSTRELS
Mary Delorme

Stella Wade's career as a concert pianist might have been ruined by the rudeness of a famous conductor, so it seemed to her agent and benefactor. Even Sir Nicholas fails to see the possibilities when John Tallis falls deeply in love with Stella.

THE TWILIGHT MAN
Frank Gruber

Jim Rand lives alone in the California desert awaiting death. Into his hermit existence comes a teenage girl who blows both his past and his brief future wide open.

DOG IN THE DARK
Gerald Hammond

Jim Cunningham breeds and trains gun dogs, and his antagonism towards the devotees of show spaniels earns him many enemies. So when one of them is found murdered, the police are on his doorstep within hours.

THE RED KNIGHT
Geoffrey Moxon

When he finds himself a pawn on the chessboard of international espionage with his family in constant danger, Guy Trent becomes embroiled in moves and countermoves which may mean life or death for Western scientists.

NURSE ALICE IN LOVE
Theresa Charles

Accepting the post of nurse to little Fernie Sherrod, Alice Everton could not guess at the romance, suspense and danger which lay ahead at the Sherrod's isolated estate.

POIROT INVESTIGATES
Agatha Christie

Two things bind these eleven stories together — the brilliance and uncanny skill of the diminutive Belgian detective, and the stupidity of his Watson-like partner, Captain Hastings.

LET LOOSE THE TIGERS
Josephine Cox

Queenie promised to find the long-lost son of the frail, elderly murderess, Hannah Jason. But her enquiries threatened to unlock the cage where crucial secrets had long been held captive.

THE LISTERDALE MYSTERY
Agatha Christie

Twelve short stories ranging from the light-hearted to the macabre, diverse mysteries ingeniously and plausibly contrived and convincingly unravelled.

TO BE LOVED
Lynne Collins

Andrew married the woman he had always loved despite the knowledge that Sarah married him for reasons of her own. So much heartache could have been avoided if only he had known how vital it was to be loved.

ACCUSED NURSE
Jane Converse

Paula found herself accused of a crime which could cost her her job, her nurse's reputation, and even the man she loved, unless the truth came to light.